THE GIRLS TAKE OVER

■ ■ ■ ■ ■

OTHER DELL YEARLING BOOKS YOU WILL ENJOY

CHARLOTTE'S ROSE, *A. E. Cannon*
QUIT IT, *Marcia Byalick*
THE TRUE PRINCE, *J. B. Cheaney*
SONG OF SAMPO LAKE, *William Durbin*
THE EGYPT GAME, *Zilpha Keatley Snyder*
SPRING-HEELED JACK, *Philip Pullman*
WHEN MY NAME WAS KEOKO, *Linda Sue Park*
EARTHBORN, *Sylvia Waugh*
THE FAIRY REBEL, *Lynne Reid Banks*
REMOTE MAN, *Elizabeth Honey*

DELL YEARLING BOOKS are designed especially to entertain and enlighten young people. Patricia Reilly Giff, consultant to this series, received her bachelor's degree from Marymount College and a master's degree in history from St. John's University. She holds a Professional Diploma in Reading and a Doctorate of Humane Letters from Hofstra University. She was a teacher and reading consultant for many years, and is the author of numerous books for young readers.

THE GIRLS
TAKE OVER

Phyllis Reynolds Naylor

A Dell Yearling Book

Published by
Dell Yearling
an imprint of
Random House Children's Books
a division of Random House, Inc.
New York

Visit us on the Web! www.randomhouse.com/kids

Educators and librarians, for a variety of teaching tools, visit us at www.randomhouse.com/teachers

ISBN: 0-440-41678-7

Reprinted by arrangement with Delacorte Press

Printed in the United States of America

March 2004

10 9 8 7 6 5 4 3 2 1

OPM

To Gretchen Corcoran

Contents

■　■　■　■　■　■

THE GIRLS TAKE OVER

■　■　■　■　■　■

One

■

Dreaming

It was the month Eddie Malloy had been waiting for—tryouts for the Buckman Elementary baseball team—only sixth graders allowed. For Caroline, however, April looked as though it might be the most boring month since they'd moved to Buckman. She didn't care much for sports, but she knew how desperately her oldest sister wanted to get on the team. What *Caroline* most wanted was for something exciting to happen to *her*—something so dramatic it would get her picture in the newspaper.

But Eddie was fuming about the rain. "*Look* at it!" she wailed, staring out at the dismal West Virginia sky. The sun, which took its sweet time rising above the hills each morning, hadn't shown for a week. "I'll bet we won't have tryouts today after all!"

Eddie, Caroline, and Beth were finishing their toast, getting ready to return to school after spring vacation.

"You've got a whole month, Eddie. The games don't

1

begin till May," Beth told her. Beth was in the fifth grade, and Caroline, being precocious, was in fourth, having been moved up a year. "Relax!" Beth said.

"I can't," said Eddie. "This is my one chance to show Jake Hatford that he's not the only good player around."

Mrs. Malloy came into the kitchen in her robe. "Gracious, I overslept!" she said. "It's a good thing you girls got yourselves up. This rain just makes me want to stay in bed. It's a good day for dreaming."

Mr. Malloy followed next and went directly to the coffeemaker. He was singing his usual song, the words being "I hate to get up in the *mooorn-ing*," and the girls rolled their eyes at each other. He was coaching Buckman College's football team this year in a teacher-exchange program. Whether or not he would move his family back to Ohio in September was still very much up in the air.

"Better wear your yellow slickers," Mrs. Malloy told the girls. "It's supposed to rain all day."

Eddie groaned and looked out the window and down the hill toward the river. The Buckman River, ordinarily shallow, was swollen now by all the rain. It entered town on one side of Island Avenue, where the family was staying, looped around under the road bridge to the business district, and went back out of Buckman again on the other side.

"Well," Eddie said finally. "If I never become a professional baseball player, I guess I'll be a scientist. That's my second choice."

"Good thinking," said her father. "Keep your bases covered." He grinned.

Beth had her nose stuck in a book as usual while she ate, her hand blindly reaching out to feel around the table for her orange juice. She never once took her eyes off the page.

"If she'd only read decent stuff!" her mother had once complained, because the stories Beth liked best were about human centipedes and creatures under the sea. Beth was currently reading a book called *The Village of the Vampire Ants*. Beth didn't give much thought to what she wanted to be when she was grown.

No one ever asked Caroline what *she* wanted to be when she grew up because she talked about it constantly: the world's greatest actress, that's what. She could see her name in lights on Broadway: *Caroline Lenore Malloy, starring in* . . . play after play after play.

■

As the Malloy girls crossed the swinging bridge that took them to College Avenue, they saw the Hatford boys waiting for them on the other side. Despite all the boys' tricks and teasing since the girls had come to Buckman, the Malloy sisters had started walking to school with them when a strange animal—which the newspaper called an abaguchie because no one knew what it was—had been sighted in the area. It had later been found to be a cougar, and the Hatford and Malloy parents had insisted their seven children walk together to and from school for protection. Now that the cougar had been caught and taken down to the Smoky Mountains, the kids, out of habit, still walked together every day.

The boys weren't exactly waiting patiently for the girls. What they were really doing was standing on the swinging bridge at their end, and as soon as the girls stepped on it, the boys began jumping up and down so that the bridge wiggled and swayed and bounced.

"Ha, ha, we're so scared!" Eddie said dryly.

"Look how high the water is!" Peter called. Peter was in second grade, the youngest of the boys. Wally was next, in fourth grade with Caroline, and the twins, Josh and Jake, were in sixth grade with Eddie. Beth was the only girl who wasn't in a class with a Hatford. *Lucky you,* Eddie had told her once.

"What's the highest the river's ever been?" Beth asked when the girls reached the other end and they all set off for school.

"It was up over the road in front of our house once," said Wally.

"Did you ever have to be rescued in rowboats or anything?" asked Caroline. She could just see herself, waving a white handkerchief from a window, the water rising to her waist, then her chest, then her throat—how she would faint just as the rescuers reached her and would have to be carried out to the boat.

"No," said Wally. "It was never that high."

Both Eddie and Jake were glum as they headed for school because Jake, too, wanted to try out for the baseball team, and they certainly couldn't do it in the rain. The rest of the crew was in good spirits, however.

"You know what we ought to do?" said Josh. "We each ought to put our name and phone number in a bottle and float them down the river. We could ask the people who find them to call and tell us where they were found, and whoever's bottle travels farthest by the end of the month wins."

"Wins what?" said Wally, who loved fooling around and liked the idea.

"Well, whoever wins could be king or queen for the day," suggested Josh.

"Queen of *what*?" asked Caroline.

"King or queen of the rest of us. The rest of us would have to be his slaves for a day and do whatever he wanted."

"Oh no you don't!" said Eddie. "If one of you guys wins, you'll make us do all kinds of gross things."

"Okay, they have to be things within reason," said Josh. "And the bottles should all be the same size. Maybe Mom could get some for us."

"Sounds fun!" said Beth.

"We'd better do it while the water's flowing fast, though," said Wally. "The bottles will go farther then."

"They might even get to the ocean!" Peter cried excitedly.

"And then one of them could be picked up by a ship at sea!" Caroline said dreamily. "I could be sitting in a chair at breakfast, calmly eating my cereal, and get a ship-to-shore message from a handsome captain of an ocean liner saying that he was coming to West Virginia to meet the maiden who had put her name in a bottle."

The others laughed.

"Or maybe he'd call to say that as soon as he read the name *Caroline Malloy*, he threw the bottle back in the ocean and washed his hands with soap and water," Jake teased.

■

It was hard to concentrate on schoolwork when there were notes to be sealed in bottles, Caroline thought. Her desk was right behind Wally Hatford's, and when she had nothing better to do, she would trace letters or words on Wally's back with the end of her ruler and dot the i's with her pencil. Or she would blow on the back of his neck and whisper romantic words, just to see his ears turn red.

But this morning she was content to stare out the window as rain trickled down the pane, and imagined a lonely aspirin bottle adrift at sea with a tiny piece of paper rolled up inside it. She imagined the handsome sea captain in his blue-and-white uniform bending over the side of the boat to scoop it up, and—

"Caroline?"

The voice of the teacher suddenly intruded, and Caroline blinked and snapped to attention.

"The answer, please?" said Miss Applebaum.

"The Ohio River?" Caroline said quickly.

"What?" said the teacher as the class turned to stare.

"The . . . the Gulf of Mexico?" Caroline bleated.

"Caroline, we happen to be doing long division, and I assure you that if you divided four thousand, six hundred and sixty-eight by twelve, you would not get the Gulf of Mexico," the teacher said. "Not even the Ohio River."

■ ■ ■ ■ ■ ■ ■ ■ ■ ■ ■ ■ ■

Two

■

A Horrible Thought

Wally took off his jacket, soaked through with rain, and hung it on a hook by the back door. He and his brothers kicked off their wet sneakers and left them in a heap against the wall.

All the way home from school that day Wally had been thinking about the bottle race they were going to have on the Buckman River. At last his brothers were going to do something that interested *him* for a change. Not dump dead birds and squirrels on the girls' side of the river. Not howl outside the Malloys' windows at night, trying to frighten them into going back to Ohio so that the Bensons would return. The Benson brothers were the best friends the Hatfords had ever had, and it had been a sad day when Coach Benson moved his family to Georgia for a year and Coach Malloy moved *his* family to Buckman. Into the Bensons' house, no less!

Putting notes in bottles to see how far they would

travel on the river was just the kind of thing Wally Hatford loved to do, however. But he couldn't help suspecting that Caroline would try to do something crazy and turn the race into a theatrical performance, starring . . . who else? Caroline Malloy!

In some ways, Wally was a loner. He could entertain himself for an hour just blowing fog on a windowpane and tracing designs in it. He could spend half an afternoon in summer lying on the porch on his stomach with his face over the side, watching ants trying to carry a bread crumb to their anthill. He seemed to live a life half in and half outside his head and didn't always need other people around to make him happy.

The boys had barely started across the kitchen when the phone rang. Wally, who was closest, picked it up. Even before the person on the line said a word, Wally said, "We're all here, Mom, and nobody's been murdered or anything."

Their mother always phoned the house as soon as she thought they'd be home from school, to be sure everyone was accounted for. She worked in a hardware store, and Mr. Hatford was a mail carrier, so the boys were on their own for a while each day after school.

"There's a little potato salad and some Swiss cheese in the fridge," Mrs. Hatford said in answer. "But don't touch the chicken. That's our dinner."

"Okay," said Wally.

"If you have any homework, now is a good time to do it, with all this rain," said his mother.

"Okay," Wally said again. Then he told her about

9

the bottle race, and Mrs. Hatford promised to bring home seven white plastic bottles with tight-fitting lids.

Jake got out the potato salad and Josh found the cheese. Peter had discovered a half-eaten box of animal crackers in his closet and was sitting at the table, swinging his legs and humming a song while he chewed.

"We should all throw our bottles into the water at the exact same time to make the race fair," said Josh, stuffing some cheese into his mouth.

Jake, however, grinned as he set a box of crackers on the table. "Who says the race has to be fair? Who says we couldn't put messages in a whole bunch of bottles and send them out on the other side of Island Avenue a day or two sooner to give them a head start?"

"That would be cheating!" said Wally.

For once, Josh agreed with him. "I don't want to do that, Jake. I'd really like to see whose bottle goes the farthest when they all begin at the same place at the same time."

Jake folded a slice of cheese over a cracker and opened a can of pop. Each boy was allowed only one can of pop a day. "Well, if my bottle goes farthest," he said, "I'm going to make everyone do my homework."

"If *I'm* King for a Day, everyone will have to do all my chores around the house," said Josh.

Wally thought about what he would most like the others to do. "If *my* bottle goes farthest, you each have to give me your can of pop for the day," he said.

"If *my* bottle wins, everybody has to bake a big, big batch of cookies all for me!" crowed Peter, beaming at the thought.

The boys chewed awhile longer, smiling as each imagined himself King for a Day. And then Wally had a thought—a terrible, awful thought. Maybe it wouldn't be a king at all. Maybe it would be a queen.

He looked around the table. "What if one of the girls' bottles goes the farthest?" he said. "What if it's Caroline's?"

The smiles disappeared from the boys' faces. If Eddie was queen, she might make them do something dangerous, like crawl high up in a tree to get a squirrel's nest. If Beth was queen, she'd probably order them to make her lunch. But if Caroline Lenore Malloy was queen, she would dress the boys in ruffled shirts and knee breeches and make them carry her down Main Street on a throne.

"We can't let that happen!" said Jake. "It would be murder!"

The phone rang again, and this time Jake answered. "Hello?" he said. Wally watched as a slow grin spread across his brother's face. "Sure!" Jake said. And then, after a minute, "Sure! Okay."

When he hung up, he said, "The girls are on their way over. Eddie wants to make some rules for the contest."

"Okay by me," said Josh.

But Jake's eyes narrowed. "How do we know the

girls aren't planning to cheat? How do we know *they* aren't going to put *their* bottles in the river ahead of ours? Eddie's up to something, you can bet."

Wally slumped down in his chair. The cracker he had been chewing stuck to the roof of his mouth. The war between the Hatfords and the Malloys would go on forever and ever, he was sure of it, until either his family or theirs left Buckman.

■ ■ ■ ■ ■ ■ ■ ■ ■ ■ ■ ■

Three

■

Deal

"What are you *saying*?" Beth asked Eddie as they sat in Beth's room after school, watching the rain stream down the second-story window.

Caroline, sitting on the floor playing jacks, thought her oldest sister was like a tiger, the way Eddie paced back and forth upstairs from one room to another. The rain made Eddie crazy.

"I just don't trust those Hatfords," Eddie said. "You *know* they're going to rig this race so that one of their bottles will get a head start. We shouldn't have agreed to this slave business."

"Oh, it might not be so bad," said Beth hopefully. "If Josh got to be king, it might be fun. Besides, what if one of *us* wins?"

"That's what we have to make happen," said Eddie. "We've got to make sure one of *our* bottles goes the farthest by April thirtieth."

Caroline's hand dropped, and the little red ball

rolled under Beth's bed. "But that would be cheating!" she said.

"So do you think that's going to stop *them*?" said Eddie. "They would never have agreed to this if they didn't know they could rig it to win."

"Then I don't want to do it if it's not a fair race," said Beth.

"If *they're* going to cheat, I'll cheat, but not if they're not," said Caroline, not quite sure of what she'd just said.

"How are we going to know?" asked Beth.

Eddie plopped down on the bed. "Here's what we'll do." She outlined a plan, and five minutes later she called the Hatford boys to say that the girls were on their way over with a contract.

In their yellow rain slickers the three Malloy sisters pulled on their boots in the kitchen.

"Where are you off to?" asked Mrs. Malloy from the dining room, where income-tax forms covered the table.

"We're just going over to the Hatfords' to make some rules for a bottle race on the river," Eddie said.

"Well, don't get too near the water," their mother called after them. "The river's starting to go down, but it's still fairly high."

"We won't," said Caroline.

The river and sky were gray, but there was a feathery fog of green on the trees—only wisps of leaves, the lightest of greens and yellows. The girls slogged down to the bridge, crossed over, and went up the sidewalk to the Hatfords' porch.

Josh opened the door. "Hi, come in," he said.

They stopped to deposit their boots on the porch. Inside, the boys were waiting for them, and Peter offered the remains of his animal crackers.

"There's a whole bear in there somewhere," he said.

"Don't eat it," Josh warned. "That box of crackers has been in Peter's closet for months, and you should see his closet!"

"You want some popcorn?" Wally offered, holding up a couple of microwave bags. That sounded more appealing, so the seven of them sat around the kitchen table listening for the popping to stop.

"Now!" said Jake.

"No . . . see, there's another pop," said Wally.

"Okay, now!" said Caroline.

"Nope. Two . . . three more pops," said Beth.

Finally the bag was removed and another inserted, and five minutes later two metal bowls of popcorn were making the rounds of the kitchen table.

"Okay, here's the deal," said Eddie. Her real name was Edith Ann, but she said she'd fight anyone who called her that. "If we're going to do the race, it's got to be fair. There are all kinds of ways we could cheat and the others wouldn't know about it, so it's got to be cheat-proof."

"How are you going to do that?" asked Wally.

"Like you said, we have to get seven bottles all the

same size, with tight caps, and we have to put them in the river at the same place at the same time," said Eddie.

Caroline looked at the faces around her as Eddie explained the rules. There was a cheating smile on Jake Hatford's face if she'd ever seen one.

"And to make sure that nobody puts the same kind of a bottle with his name and address in it a day or so early," she continued, which made Jake suddenly snap to attention, "the girls get to put something secret in each of the boys' bottles, and the boys get to do the same with the girls' bottles. This way, if someone calls us to say that they found one of our bottles, we'll ask what was in it, and it had better have the secret something or we'll know it's an extra bottle somebody put in the river, and that won't count."

The boys looked at each other.

"Okay," said Jake finally. "Fair enough."

"I could find something secret to put in our bottles!" Peter offered helpfully.

"Peter, anything you find in your closet will be either moldy or decayed," said Josh. "No thanks."

"Are we agreed on the time limit?" Eddie went on.

"Four weeks," said Jake. "The deadline will be the last day of April. Whoever's bottle goes farthest by then gets to make the others do what he says."

"Or *she* says," put in Beth.

"Yeah," said Jake.

"But wait!" said Wally. "What if someone finds one of the bottles but doesn't call?"

"There's nothing we can do about that. It's just the chance we have to take," said Eddie. "And if they call after April thirtieth, too bad." She put up her hand. "Deal?"

"Deal," said Jake, slapping her palm.

The girls walked all around the table giving high fives to the boys, the butter from the popcorn traveling hand to hand. Then they went to the front door to put on their boots and raincoats.

"Hey, look! Sun!" said Beth.

It wasn't sun exactly, but the sky was brighter and the rain had stopped. For the first time in days there was a little gold in the sky along with the gray.

"Maybe they'll hold tryouts tomorrow," Eddie mused.

"Goodbye, Eddie! Goodbye, Beth and Caroline!" called Peter, holding one of the popcorn bowls in his arms and scooping up the last kernels.

"Goodbye," said Caroline. "Get ready to be my humble, obedient slaves if my bottle goes the farthest."

"Ha!" shot back Jake. "Be ready to work like dogs if *my* bottle goes the farthest."

The girls crossed the road and went down the path to the swinging bridge, stopping to peer over the cable handrail at the water.

"Do you suppose it's over our heads now?" Caroline asked.

"In places, I suppose. The guys said there are only certain parts of it deep enough for swimming," said Beth.

"Still, I'll bet a bottle would travel pretty fast in this," mused Eddie aloud.

"I wonder what it's like to be in a flood," said Caroline. "Just think if water was slowly creeping up your stairs, and you had to crawl out a window onto the roof and wave a pillowcase at passersby, pleading for help, and a helicopter came along and a handsome man dropped a rope ladder and he crawled down and picked you up in his arms and climbed back up the ladder and—"

"Okay, Caroline, we get the picture," said Eddie. "Everything to you is just a movie. If you *were* in a real tragedy, it wouldn't seem so romantic."

"I can do tragic!" said Caroline. "What if a woman crawled out on the roof with her little baby in her arms, but the water kept rising and rushing, and swept the baby away and—"

"Stop it!" said Beth. "Caroline, can't you just talk normal for a change?"

The girls went on across the bridge and up the soggy hill to their house.

"I don't want to leave here," said Caroline. "We've had more fun in Buckman than we ever had back in Ohio."

"Well, I don't think we're going to have any say in it, whatever Dad decides," Eddie told her.

In the kitchen they took off their wet clothes.

"Sun's trying to come out," called their mother. "The forecast says it's supposed to clear up for a while."

That was good news—for Eddie, anyway.

"Mom," said Caroline, going to the door of the dining room. "Has Dad said anything more about going back to Ohio? Do you think we will?"

"My dear, you know as much about it as I do," Mrs. Malloy said. "He's waiting to hear from someone who's waiting to hear from someone else who's waiting to hear . . . It's like dominoes. I wouldn't be surprised if we don't find out till the very last minute. With your father, anything could happen!"

Four

■

Tryouts

Mrs. Hatford brought home the seven bottles as requested, but on Tuesday the rain had stopped, so the Big Bottle Race was put on hold till the team had been chosen. After school Jake Hatford and Eddie Malloy were both out on the school baseball diamond with the other hopefuls. They had all been practicing for an hour under the watchful eye of their coach, and finally he called everyone over. They were all boys except for Eddie.

"With only nine players on a team," Mr. Bailey said, "I have to make a choice and choose the nine of you for the A team that I think will play best. The rest of you will be the B team, and you'll each be a substitute for an A player. Things happen in a game, you know. If a player gets sick or hurt, a substitute has to be ready to take over, so you'll come to every practice too. Some of you may even prove to be better players than my A team, and I'll keep watching you during practice. If I need to change you around, I will, so everyone needs to play his very best."

All the boys, of course, were looking sideways at Eddie. So were all of Jake's brothers and Eddie's two sisters, who sat on the wooden bleachers behind home plate.

The coach went down the line and chose the nine players for the A team. Both Eddie and Jake made the list, to the cheers of those in the bleachers. Then Mr. Bailey asked each of the nine what position he would most like to play.

"Pitcher," said Jake.

"Pitcher," said Eddie.

Some of the boys smiled and elbowed each other. Baseball was big in Buckman, and half the kids in the school—the boys, anyway—wanted to be one of the Buckman Badgers when they reached sixth grade. Four on the A team wanted to be the pitcher, and Mr. Bailey tried them out one by one till only Jake and Eddie were left.

"Who wants to go first?" asked Mr. Bailey.

Jake and Eddie both said, "I will," at the same time.

"Okay," the coach said. "Jake, you pick up a bat there, and Edith Ann, you—"

"Eddie," she corrected firmly.

"Okay, Eddie. You go out to the mound." The coach tossed her a ball, and Eddie took her place.

The Hatford brothers and the Malloy sisters were all rooting for both Jake and Eddie for a change, because they wouldn't be competing against each other; they'd be playing teams from other schools.

"Okay, let's see what you can do," the coach said.

Eddie juggled the ball around in her hands a couple of times. The other boys, whom Mr. Bailey had sent out in the field to catch, laughed softly among themselves.

Jake chose a bat, and after a few practice swings went to home plate. Mr. Bailey served as catcher.

"Ready?" the coach called out.

Eddie drew back her arm, her body turning a little to one side. She slowly lifted one foot off the ground, and then, *pow!* The ball came so fast that Jake wasn't ready. He blinked as the boys in the outfield fell silent. Mr. Bailey caught the ball and sent it back to Eddie.

"Good throw!" he said. "Let's see another one."

This time Jake was ready. With his knees slightly bent, weight on the balls of his feet, he gripped the bat, his eyes on Eddie. He saw her arm move back, saw her body turn, saw her foot come off the ground, and then the pitch. *Crack!*

The ball went sailing out over left field and was caught by one of Jake's friends.

"Good! Good pitch! Good swing, Jake! Now, you two trade places."

There were murmurs in the outfield again, and the boys automatically moved in a little closer to catch any ball Eddie might hit.

Jake did his windup with a flourish and let the ball fly.

Crack!

The ball sailed out over Jake's head, far out into center field, and rolled along the ground several yards before a fielder could rush back to scoop it up.

"Again!" the coach said.

Wally could tell from the way Jake was winding up this time that he was trying to scare Eddie. *Whish* came the ball, but Eddie was faster. She didn't even blink.

Crack!

The ball sailed out over right field.

"Get it! Get it!" the boys were yelling, but Eddie could have made a home run in the time it took them to get the ball back to Mr. Bailey.

"Okay, Eddie, you're in," said the coach. "So are you, Jake. I'm going to have you two trade off as pitchers."

Over on the bleachers the Hatford and Malloy cheering sections hooted and hollered.

When both the A and B teams finished practice an hour later, the Hatfords and the Malloys walked home together. It seemed to Wally that Beth and Caroline just wouldn't shut up about how well Eddie had performed. They didn't say anything about Jake.

"You *did* it! You *did* it! You made the team!" Caroline cried, slapping her sister on the back.

"Boy, you showed them!" said Beth. "Mr. Bailey's

teeth almost fell out when he saw you hit that first ball. You're *in,* Eddie! You're *in*! You'll wow 'em!"

"I *told* them I could do it!" Eddie crowed. "I wish the games began this month. I wish we didn't have to wait till May."

"Everybody needs practice," Jake mumbled. "Even you."

■

When they had parted at last at the swinging bridge and the Malloy girls had gone home, Jake said to the others, "She'll be impossible, you know."

"She already is," said Wally.

"Who?" asked Peter.

"The Whomper, of course!" said Jake. That was the nickname they'd given Eddie. "It'll go to her head! You can tell already. Did you hear how many times she kept saying, 'I *told* everyone I could pitch! I *told* everyone I could bat!' So okay, already! Do we have to go on hearing that the rest of the season?"

Wally didn't say so, but Jake sounded a little jealous.

"Just be glad she's on your team and not playing for some other school," Josh said.

"Yeah," said Jake, but he didn't look very happy about it.

■

At dinner that evening, when Jake announced he'd made the A team, Mrs. Hatford said, "That's great, Jake! Didn't you try out, Josh?" People often thought that Josh and Jake, being twins, liked the same things. Even their parents made that mistake sometimes.

"No," said Josh, who was a sort of resident artist for the school. He could draw better than anyone in Buckman Elementary, including the teachers. "I'll just watch from the bleachers."

"The parents are going to take turns driving you kids to the Saturday games next month," Mr. Hatford said. "Your mother and I will each take a Saturday off if we need to, and I'm sure the Malloys will do their share of driving."

"Of course!" said Jake. "They wouldn't want to miss seeing their precious Edith Ann pulverize the other team, would they?" He jabbed at his potato and stuffed a bite into his mouth.

Mrs. Hatford studied him. "Do you *mind* having Eddie on your team?" she asked.

"Heck, no," Jake insisted. "As long as she doesn't throw her weight around when she's with us, I'm okay with it." And he jabbed his potato again.

But next to throwing a baseball, throwing her weight around seemed to be what Eddie did best. When they all walked to school together the next day, she made a point of telling them that she was wearing her backpack on her left shoulder only because it was important not to put any stress on her pitching arm.

When they stood on the playground waiting for the

bell, she did finger exercises because, she said, it was important to keep her fingers flexible.

When she had to write an essay on the topic of her choice for sixth-grade English, Eddie chose "The History of Baseball," Jake told Wally at recess. "She needs to be taken down a peg," he said.

Uh-oh, thought Wally. Whenever Jake talked like that, it meant trouble.

As all seven of them walked home together that afternoon, talking baseball, Wally said, to change the subject, "We'd better do that bottle race today. The water's already going down."

It was true that although they still couldn't see the rocks that lay in clumps in the riverbed, the river wasn't as high as it had been only a few days before.

"All right," said Eddie. "We'll go home and find something secret to go in your bottles. Then we'll be over."

"Why don't we follow the river back as far as we can before we throw the bottles in?" Jake suggested. "Then we can watch them pass by our house, go down around the bend, and float back up the other side of Island Avenue."

"Unless they get stuck upriver somewhere," said Wally. "The river twists and turns a lot before it gets to our house."

"We decided to paint the caps on our bottles red," said Josh. "That way we can tell them from yours, Eddie, and see which ones are ahead. Just for fun."

Wally saw Eddie's eyes narrow. "Are you sure that's the only reason?" she asked.

"Of course!" said Jake. "What other reason could there be?"

"Ha!" said Beth.

"Double ha!" said Caroline.

■ ■ ■ ■ ■ ■ ■ ■ ■ ■ ■

Five

■

Into the Drink

"**Y**ou just *know* they're up to something!" said Eddie, once the girls were home.

Caroline and Beth had to agree.

"They didn't paint those bottle caps red for nothing!" said Beth. "I'll bet they're going to sneak around to the other side of Island Avenue where we can't see them and try to fish out our bottles as they go by."

"Maybe they won't be able to reach them," said Caroline.

"And maybe they *will*!" said Eddie. "You know what? We'll just have to fish theirs out first! And they've made it easy for us to tell which ones are theirs."

"They've ruined it all!" said Beth, disappointed. "I don't want to win by cheating."

"We're just saving our own skins, beating the boys at their own game," Eddie told her. Her eyes began to gleam. "Do you know what's up in the loft of our garage?"

Caroline thought. "Window screens," she said. That was all she could remember.

"What else?" said Eddie, her eyes becoming little slits. They looked almost like cat's eyes.

"Boxes? Dry leaves? Pigeon poop?"

"What else?" said Eddie, and when neither Caroline nor Beth could guess, she said, "A butterfly net."

Caroline remembered. There was indeed an old pole with a net at the end.

"Perfect!" said Beth, finally enthusiastic about their plan. "Absolutely perfect! Are we in charge or *what*?"

When the girls got to the Hatfords', they found seven white bottles on the kitchen table, four with caps painted red and three with white caps. Each person was to put a slip of paper in a bottle, giving his or her name and phone number. Wally helped Peter with his.

"You know," Caroline said, looking up, "maybe we ought to write a little more on our slips of paper, saying how important it is that people call us before the end of April. Otherwise, maybe nobody will bother."

That seemed like a good idea, so there was more writing and erasing.

When all the girls' messages had been written, rolled, and thrust down into the bottles with the white caps and the boys' messages had been thrust down into the bottles with the red caps, they exchanged bottles. They turned their backs on each other, and Eddie reached into her jeans pocket and pulled out four buttons off an old Girl Scout uniform. She dropped one button in each of the boys' bottles and put the caps back on.

Jake reached into the pocket of his faded denim jacket and pulled out three matchbook covers from a Mexican restaurant in Parkersburg. He bent each matchbook cover until it would go through the neck of each of the girls' bottles. Then he put the white caps back on the bottles.

When everyone had his or her own bottle back, each screwed on the cap as tightly as possible and sealed it with candle wax.

"Ready?" said Josh.

"Ready," said the girls.

They put on their jackets again and started up the road outside the Hatfords' house, going in the opposite direction from school. College Avenue began downtown by the college and ran out past the Hatfords' house, on and on, following the Buckman River, until finally, about a mile away, it began to veer off from the water and ended at last at the highway.

The kids decided they would follow the avenue down to where it left the river, and there they would throw the bottles in, then walk back home to the swinging bridge and watch the bottles float by.

"Wouldn't it be wild if one of our bottles was swept out into the Atlantic and bobbed around for years before anyone found it?" said Jake.

"Wouldn't it be weird if one of us was shipwrecked, and one day one of our own bottles washed up on shore?" said Caroline.

As they followed the road, there were times when they could see the river and times when they couldn't, for it wound and twisted and curved before it came back to amble along the road again. At last they came to the bend in College Avenue where the road left the river for good. The seven of them left the road and walked along the ground until they were close enough to the water to toss their bottles in. The air had been mild for the past few days, and the kids were warm inside their jackets.

"Okay, who wants to go first?" asked Eddie. And then, answering her own question, she pulled back her arm and, with an underhand pitch, sent her bottle sailing out into the very middle of the river. The bottle disappeared for a moment, and then they saw the white cap bobbing slowly along the surface, beginning its long journey down the Buckman River, and everyone cheered.

Jake and Josh threw next, then Beth, then Wally, then Caroline, and finally Peter. Peter's bottle landed only a few feet from the bank beside an old rubber tire, so Wally reached out with a stick and retrieved it, and Jake threw it in again for his brother.

"Well, there they go," said Josh.

" 'Luck, be a lady tonight!' " Jake called, a line from a song his dad used to sing, and everyone laughed.

"Goodbye!" called Caroline.

"Happy landing!" said Beth.

"May the best bottle win," said Wally, and they laughed some more.

They climbed back up the bank and made their way over to College Avenue again, heading home.

When they reached the swinging bridge, Jake said, "You know, it's going to take those bottles forever to get here, and we're going to have dinner soon. I don't think I'll wait around to watch them go by."

"I'm tired," said Peter. "I want to go in."

"Yeah, me too," said Josh.

And when the boys began walking up toward their house, Eddie said, "We're leaving too. I've got a ton of homework."

"So have I," said Beth.

"See you!" they all said to each other, and then the Hatfords went up on their porch and the girls started across the bridge.

"I thought you said you didn't have any homework tonight," Caroline said to Eddie.

"I don't!" said Eddie. "But we've got a job to do anyway. Didn't you notice how Jake was trying to make us believe he wasn't interested in watching the bottles go by after all? That's because he doesn't want *us* to be around when they do. I'll bet they're going to come out later. They know we could see them from our upstairs windows if they tried to fish our bottles out here by the bridge. I figure they'll wait until they think the bottles will reach the other side of Island Avenue, and then they'll go pull our bottles out as they go by over there."

"The dogs!" said Caroline.

"And here's what *we're* going to do!" said Eddie. "I'm getting the butterfly net from the garage. We'll take it

32

down under the swinging bridge and fish *their* bottles out first."

"But *they'll* see *us*!" Caroline said.

"Not if we can get over the bridge first and down the bank on their side. They could see us from their upstairs windows if we tried to do it over here, but the bank's steep enough on their side that it will hide us."

"So we'll fish out their bottles, and they'll fish out ours, and there won't be any bottles at all finishing the race," said Beth.

"I guess that's about it," said Eddie. "Better no race at all than us getting humiliated and having to be their slaves."

"But they'll see us crossing the bridge with the butterfly net!" said Caroline, still wondering if Eddie's idea would work.

"Yeah, that's the hard part," Eddie agreed. She was quiet a moment. "Okay, here's what we'll do: Beth and I will go first, and Caroline, you walk right behind us with the net, hiding it if you can. If we can just make it to the other side, they won't be able to see us anymore from their windows."

Eddie got the net, and off they went.

"Now, walk close to me, Beth, so our shoulders touch," Eddie instructed, "and, Caroline, try to keep the pole hidden behind us, if you can, as we cross the bridge. As soon as we get to the other side, slide down the bank and out of sight. Okay?"

The three girls went down to the footbridge again, Caroline trying to hold the long pole so that it could not be seen from an upstairs window of the Hatfords' house. This was hard to do.

At least the boys were all inside now. That was in the girls' favor. The wooden planks bounced as they walked, and it was hard to move all stuck together.

"Look!" Beth said suddenly. "I see the bottles! Two white caps and a red one!"

"Hurry!" said Eddie.

They reached the other side and went sliding down the muddy bank to the river, out of sight of the Hatfords' upstairs windows.

"Here comes a bottle!" cried Beth. "Give me the pole, Caroline."

But Caroline was already out on a large rock that extended into the water. "I'll get it, I'll get it!" she said.

"Ouch!" said Eddie as the end of the pole hit her on the head. "Be careful, Caroline! Give the pole to Beth. Her arms are longer."

"No, I'll get it! I'll get it!" Caroline cried, leaning out as far as she could.

And then, of course, it happened. Where Caroline was concerned, anything could. She felt her left foot slip, her right foot slide, and with a little shriek, she plunged face first into the river.

Six

■

Double Cross

Mrs. Hatford was home when the boys reached the house. Peter went into the kitchen to get a snack. Jake grabbed Josh and Wally by the arms and rushed them upstairs where their mother couldn't hear.

"If we go back to the river, I'll bet we'll see those bottles come by, and we can grab the girls' bottles and pull them out."

"That's cheating!" said Wally. "I thought this was going to be a real race."

"*I* thought you just wanted to bring Eddie down a peg or two. I don't know why you want to punish Beth," said Josh, who rather liked the middle Malloy girl.

"Well, if I knew which bottle was Eddie's, I wouldn't have to take them all. Tell you what—if I pull out either Caroline's or Beth's, I'll toss it back in."

"How are you going to know which is which without opening them up? And if you open one up, it won't be waterproof anymore," said Wally.

"Tough luck," said Jake.

"But how are you going to get them out of the river?" Wally could see it now. They'd make him put on Dad's hip-high fishing boots, take the fishnet, and wade out into the water. No! This time he would not do it! He simply wouldn't!

"I'm not going to wade out in the river with Dad's hip boots and fishnet," he said boldly and firmly. "If you want Eddie's bottle, you have to get it yourself."

Jake studied him for a moment. "Okay, okay. Don't have a spaz," he said.

"We'd be nuts to try to fish them out on this side of Island Avenue anyway. The girls could see us from their house," said Josh. "If we wait till the bottles go around the bend, the river's shallower on the other side of the island."

"Yeah, but we'd still need Dad's boots," said Jake.

"And fishnet," said Josh. "Where are they?"

They both looked at Wally. Now was his chance to say nothing. Was it possible only he knew that they were in the attic? Why were they looking at him like that?

"Wal-ly?" said Jake, slowly advancing toward him. "Where does Dad keep his hip boots and net?"

Wally's lips were dry and stuck together as the words came out. "The attic. *But I'm not going to wade out there and get Eddie's bottle!*"

"Okay. Just crawl up in the attic for us and find

them," said Josh. "We'll cover for you in case Mom wants to know where you are. But hurry!"

This always happened! Wally always got in trouble because of the twins. The only way to stay out of trouble in the Hatford house was to separate himself from Jake and Josh entirely. He wondered if a fourth-grade boy could just walk into the county courthouse and ask for a divorce from his older brothers. A legal paper he could carry around in his pocket that said they weren't related.

Jake and Josh went out in the hall and listened at the top of the stairs to be sure no one was coming, then motioned to Wally to open the small door to the attic and climb the narrow stairs.

It was dark and cobwebby in the attic. Above Wally's head was a trapdoor leading out to the widow's walk on top of the house—a kind of balcony where the wife of a sea captain would stand, searching the horizon for her husband's ship, hoping he wasn't lost at sea. Why anyone would build a widow's walk on top of a house in Buckman, West Virginia, Wally didn't know, because the closest a ship had ever come to their town was the Ohio River, and that was a long way off.

Wally rummaged along the wall, sorting through old hammocks, inner tubes, trunks, and garment bags, but he couldn't see any of his father's fishing gear. Maybe it was in the basement. Maybe it wasn't in the attic at all.

He went to the little window, where the light was

better. Maybe the boots were in the bags and boxes piled there. He caught sight of Eddie and Beth coming across the swinging bridge, their bodies stuck strangely together at the shoulders as though they were glued. But stranger yet, something stuck out behind them that looked as though Eddie had a tail!

Wally hurried back down the narrow stairs.

"Hey!" he said. "Eddie's got a tail."

"What?" said Jake. "Where are the boots? What are you talking about?"

"I couldn't find the boots, but I looked out the window, and Eddie's coming across the bridge. She's got a tail!"

The three boys ran to the window in the twins' bedroom. There, coming across the swinging bridge, were Beth and Eddie, walking side by side, and sticking out behind Eddie, just as Wally had said, was a tail. A long straight tail, like a pointer.

"Didn't I *tell* you she was a devil?" Jake joked, still mystified.

"Yeah, but one of the girls has an extra pair of feet," said Josh, leaning closer to the window and staring hard. "That's not a tail, Wally, it's a pole. Somebody's walking behind them, carrying a pole!"

"Caroline!" said Jake and Wally together.

As the boys watched, they saw the girls glance hurriedly up toward their house as they reached the edge of the bridge and then go slipping and sliding down the bank, as though trying to keep Caroline and what she was carrying hidden from view.

"What are they up to?" asked Josh.

"Guess!" said Jake. "Look again! I'll bet anything that's a butterfly net Caroline's got in her hands. Why, those double-crossing cheats! They're going to fish our bottles out of the river!"

"And those red caps we put on our bottles make it easy for them!" said Josh. "Our bottles are sitting ducks!"

"Yeah, but *we* were going to pull out *their* bottles!" said Wally, trying to make sense of the war that had suddenly heated up a notch.

The three boys started to bolt from the room, but Jake abruptly stopped and put one finger to his lips. "Where's Peter? Don't let Peter come along. He'd blab like anything."

"He's in the kitchen with Mom; I can hear them," said Josh.

"Where's Dad? Shouldn't he be home by now?"

"I think he's on duty this evening," said Josh. Besides being a mail carrier, Mr. Hatford was an assistant deputy sheriff in Buckman, and three times a week he manned the telephone in the small sheriff's office.

The boys crept downstairs and put their jackets on, avoiding the second step from the bottom, which creaked if you stepped on it. They slowly opened the front door, closed it again behind them, and started to run across the road.

This time Josh stopped them. "Don't let them see us. What we want to do is catch them red-handed. If we accuse them before they get any of our bottles, we won't be able to prove a thing."

They crept behind a clump of serviceberry bushes and slowly, slowly raised their heads until just their eyes were showing above the tops of the branches.

What they saw made even Wally lose his faith in human honesty, for there were Beth and Eddie, running along the bank upstream, their eyes on the water, their fingers pointing toward the river, where not one, not two, but three of the boys' red-capped bottles were bobbing along on the current. And there was Caroline, teetering on a large rock that jutted out into the water. She was holding a pole with a net on the end of it.

"That's a butterfly net, all right!" said Josh. "Man oh man! They are cheats through and through."

"Give me the pole, Caroline," they heard Beth say.

"I'll get it! I'll get it!" Caroline kept saying, maneuvering around on the rock.

"Ouch!" said Eddie as the end of the pole hit her on the head. "Be careful, Caroline! Give the net to Beth. Her arms are longer."

"No, I'll get it! I'll get it!" Caroline cried, leaning out as far as she could.

And then it happened so fast that Wally could hardly believe what he saw, what he heard.

A little shriek, a grunt, and just as Beth and Eddie lunged forward to grab their sister, a splash.

The three boys shot up like rockets, their mouths hanging open, as Beth and Eddie scrambled up on the rock. But Caroline was already in the river, her puffy nylon jacket scrunched up around her neck, her arms rigid—and she was moving steadily downstream.

"The pole! Hand us the end of the pole!" Eddie yelled. But Caroline's eyes were huge. The pole had sunk down under the surface and only the net was visible on top. The space between the net and Caroline grew wider and wider, and the boys could tell she wasn't holding on to it at all.

Beth screamed, and at once the three Hatford boys came tumbling down the bank, running alongside the river to see if they could get to the bend where the channel narrowed, to grab Caroline there. Eddie and Beth were at their heels.

"Hey, listen," Jake yelled over his shoulder, "she could stand up if she really tried."

"Are you sure?" cried Eddie.

"Yeah, the only deep parts are on beyond Buckman," said Josh. "Stand up, Caroline!" he yelled.

Out in the water Caroline suddenly seemed to come alive. She began flailing her arms, trying to grab hold of something. When a small tree limb floated by, she wrapped one arm around that.

"Hold on, Caroline!" Eddie yelled. "We'll catch you going around the bend!"

"Just stand up!" Josh bellowed again. "It's not that deep! Stand up!"

Caroline, however, still holding on to the limb, simply lay back in the water and closed her eyes.

"Look at her!" Jake said. "She's not even trying!"

"Maybe the branch hit her on the head," suggested

41

Wally. Surely someone would see them, he kept telling himself. There weren't a lot of cars out around dinnertime on a Wednesday evening, but *someone* in a car going over the road bridge ahead would certainly glance down and see a girl in the water and five kids racing along the bank.

But the path by the river gave way to heavy brush and brambles. Trees were closing in. Caroline was moving farther and farther away from them, and when she reached the bend, she bobbed along under the road bridge and disappeared.

"The other side!" Eddie yelled. "We've got to cross Island Avenue and get her when she comes around over there. Oh, when I get my hands on my *sister . . .*!"

■ ■ ■ ■ ■ ■ ■ ■ ■ ■ ■ ■

Seven

■

Rescue

When Caroline first hit the water, the shock made her suck in her breath. She was in the river! She was being swept away! Except for the puffy jacket, which ballooned up around her neck like a life preserver, the rest of her clothes were filling with water and dragging her down. For the first sixty seconds or so, she was utterly terrified. Then one foot scraped along the bottom and she realized she could probably walk out if she really tried.

But why try? The water was cold, but not icy, and she felt sure she could stand it for another five minutes anyway. She was fascinated to see Beth and Eddie running along the bank, screaming for her to hand them the pole. The pole? The butterfly net? She tried to turn her head, to find the pole, but only the net was visible, and even it seemed to be slowly sinking.

Now Jake and Josh and Wally were tumbling down the bank, running toward Beth and Eddie, yelling for

Caroline to stand up, but all the while she was being carried farther and farther downstream toward the road bridge, where the river turned. She would soon be out of sight. Was this the moment she had been waiting for ever since they moved to Buckman, the start of her glorious career? She summoned all her concentration on the plot that was unfolding before her and tried to adopt a look of terror and despair.

Oh, was this the end? Would she never be on Broadway? Was the name Caroline Lenore Malloy never to be in lights on a marquee? She tried to look desperate. She tried to look pitiful. No, no, she *had* to live! She managed a fake sob and began to flail her arms, just as she was bonked on the forehead by a limb floating downriver beside her.

She was able to drape one arm over the limb, and she felt her other foot scrape the bottom. Caroline was an excellent swimmer, so she had never been afraid of water. She'd just never been in water with all her clothes on.

This could be her finest hour! Her name would be in all the papers along with her picture! On the front page of the *Buckman Herald,* beneath a banner headline, *CAROLINE RESCUED!* readers would see the almost lifeless form of a young girl, one limp arm draped over a branch, her beautiful hair spread out over the surface of the water, her face pale, eyes closed. Her white skin would make readers cry, her blue lips would bring a sob to their throats. . . .

Her eyelids fluttered a moment. Were newspaper photos in color? Oh, they had to be! It would be so much more dramatic if she was in color!

Her teeth chattered, but as long as she had a limb to hang on to, she wasn't about to take off her jacket and swim. And she certainly wasn't going to ruin the drama by simply standing up and walking out of the river. No, she would at least let it carry her around to the other side of Island Avenue and hope that a crowd would be waiting. She could see her sisters and the Hatford boys back on the bank, trying to get beyond the tangle of brush and bushes blocking their path.

She looked around in dismay. Where was the photographer? Why weren't there people standing on the road bridge, calling down to her to have courage? Where were the sirens? The police? The fire department? Could it possibly be that for this, her best performance yet, there was to be no audience at all? No applauding when she was rescued? No encore?

Caroline waved her free hand weakly in the air.

"Help! Help!" she cried as tragically as she could. "Pleeeease, won't someone save me?"

Another car went by on the bridge up ahead but didn't stop.

This is ridiculous! thought Caroline. There was no point being in rushing water if no one was around to appreciate it. What would an actress do if she was in a play and nobody came?

Well, if she was ever in a movie and the script called

for her to be washed overboard, she would remember how cold, clammy clothes felt against her body, how her wet hair clung to the side of her face.

Bam! Bump! Her bottom banged against a rock beneath the surface.

"Ow!" cried Caroline as her knee hit a rock.

"Help!" she cried pitifully. "Oh, somebody save me! Pleeeease . . . !"

Blub, blub. A swell of water filled her mouth and flooded her face as she was carried around the bend in the river. Maybe she *should* just try to stand up and wade out. She passed through the shadow of the road bridge and moved along the opposite side of Island Avenue. If she wasn't rescued soon, this whole scene would have been for nothing.

She was facing upstream now, the current turning her first one way, then another. And in that moment, looking back toward the bridge, she saw a car stop. She saw a woman get out and run to the bridge railing. The woman was holding a cell phone to her ear, and Caroline felt sure she was calling 911.

Yes! An audience at last! And just in time, too, because her wet clothes felt like cement around her body, and her teeth were chattering.

Another swell of water caught her in the mouth and the current spun her around again. And there, up ahead, she saw a wall. A wall of people in purple parkas and blue ski jackets.

Five children and two men were standing waist deep

in the water, their hands locked together, as Caroline came bumping and bobbing along.

"Here she comes!" she heard Eddie yell. "Caroline, can't you stand up?"

And a man called, "Don't let her slip between you."

"Goodbye, cruel world!" Caroline cried, tipping back again and closing her eyes to the sky.

The next thing she knew, she was turning facedown as she bumped against Jake Hatford's legs, and then she opened her eyes and saw a big burly man charging through the river toward her, water spraying out around him as he grabbed her jacket, then her arm, and hauled her through the water toward the bank. The other man herded the rest of the kids after them.

They all collapsed on the bank, their chests heaving. Caroline opened one eye just enough to see a rescue vehicle, its lights flashing, up on Island Avenue.

"You kids are darned lucky we were coming by just now," the second man said, wringing water out of his pant legs. "Why didn't one of you go call 911?"

"There wasn't time! We hoped someone would see us and call the fire department," Beth said. Caroline realized why Beth was going along with the act: to divert the boys' attention from what the girls had been doing down by the river with a butterfly net in the first place.

A siren sounded in the distance, but a man from the rescue vehicle was already running toward the little group on the bank.

The burly man who had pulled Caroline out turned to the others. "You kids better get on some dry clothes," he said.

Never mind the others, Caroline was thinking. *What about me, the almost-drowned?*

As a fire engine stopped on the road above, Caroline rolled over on her back, her arms outstretched.

"What have you got?" a fireman yelled, running toward them.

"A girl was in the river, but we pulled her out," the burly man said.

"What about the other kids?" asked the fireman.

"They helped rescue her. We're all okay, I think." He looked at Caroline uncertainly.

Then another car door slammed, and Caroline heard Mr. Hatford's voice: "Don't *tell* me . . . !"

"Yep, Tom. Looks like it's your boys again. I don't know if they hunt for trouble or trouble hunts for them, but this time they were the rescuers, I hear," the fireman said. "Got a girl who fell in the river, but they're all okay."

"Who was it?" Mr. Hatford asked his sons, and they all three pointed to Caroline. Mr. Hatford groaned.

The rescue worker was kneeling beside Caroline. "You okay, sweetheart?" he asked.

Caroline didn't answer.

He reached for her wrist and felt her pulse. Caroline let her eyelids flutter. "Are you okay?" he asked again.

No answer.

"If she was in the river, she probably got bounced

around a little," Mr. Hatford suggested. "Looks like she got a bump there on her forehead."

"Can you tell me your name?" the rescue worker asked Caroline.

"Juliet," she whispered.

Jake and Josh and Wally and Eddie and Beth all stared.

"Juliet what?" the rescue worker said.

"Shakespeare," said Caroline breathily.

"Caroline!" yelled Eddie.

"Do you know what year it is?" one of the firemen asked as the men gathered around the limp wet figure on the ground.

Caroline tried to remember the year William Shakespeare was born. "Fifteen . . . uh . . . sixty-four," she said.

"Car-o-line!" the Hatford boys all yelled together.

"Hit her on the head again, Mr. Hatford," said Eddie. "I think you'll discover she's fine."

"How did this happen?" Mr. Hatford asked.

"We saw Caroline fall in the river and couldn't reach her. She had hold of a limb, so we ran around to the other side of Island Avenue to catch her when she came by here. We flagged down these men on the road to help us," said Wally.

"Good thinking," one of the firemen said. "But next time have somebody call 911. You kids were lucky today, but you never know about a river. If we hadn't gotten a call from a woman on the bridge, or these men hadn't happened along, no telling how this day might have ended. Where do you live?" he asked the girls. "We'll get you home."

"No!" Eddie said quickly, not wanting her parents to see the ruckus they had caused. "We're in that white house right down there. We'll walk. Come on, Caroline." She and Beth pulled their younger sister to her feet. Water oozed from their clothes.

"I'll follow along behind them," Mr. Hatford told the firemen. He motioned to his boys to get into his car. Turning to the Malloy girls, he asked, "What were you doing so close to the water in the first place?"

"Yeah, Eddie, what were you guys doing down by the river with a butterfly net?" said Jake.

But Caroline interrupted. "Is this London?" she asked faintly. "Am I on Drury Lane?"

"Caroline, shut up," said Beth, and without a word to the boys she and Eddie grabbed their sister by the arms and led her home.

■ ■ ■ ■ ■ ■ ■ ■ ■ ■ ■ ■

Eight

■

Conversation with Caroline

"Just *forget* those girls!" Jake growled the next day, when baseball practice was scheduled for after school. "Every time we get mixed up with the Malloys, we get in trouble."

"You can't exactly forget Eddie if she's playing on your team," said Josh.

"Don't remind me," said Jake. "All I'm going to think about from now till school's out is baseball."

"I could be your ball boy!" said Peter hopefully. "Every time you miss a ball, I could pick it up for you!"

"That's the catcher's job, Peter," said Jake.

"Well, I could be your water boy, then. Every time you come off the field, I could give you a drink of water."

Jake gave him a little smile. "All I need is for you guys to be there on the bleachers cheering every time the Buckman Badgers make a run. You can even cheer for Eddie. What I *don't* want is to get in some kind of trouble and get kicked off the team. That's why I'm not getting near the Malloys if I can help it."

What Jake was talking about, of course, was the story that had appeared in the newspaper that morning about the dramatic rescue of Caroline Malloy. How the brave Hatford boys and the courageous Malloy sisters had linked arms and caught the youngest Malloy girl as she came down the river on the far side of Island Avenue. There was no photo, but all the kids had their names in the paper, as though they were heroes.

Their parents didn't quite see it that way, however.

"The darn most foolish harebrained stunt I ever saw!" Mr. Hatford had fumed to his sons. "How you kids manage to make a bottle race a major event is beyond me."

The girls had been grounded for a week, with the exception of school and baseball practice. Coach Malloy had ruefully declared—jokingly, of course—that he was going to lock his daughters in the attic to keep them out of trouble.

Wally crawled up in the bleachers beside Josh and Peter while Jake joined the other team members on the field.

Sports weren't exactly Wally's thing. If Jake's team won a game, that was fine with Wally. If they lost, that was fine too. Sitting on cold bleachers watching baseball practice, not even a real game, was way, way down on the list of things Wally liked to do, but if he didn't come to practice, he wouldn't be part of the dinner-table discussion at night, for Mr. Hatford enjoyed sports very much and liked to hear how practice had gone. If Wally wasn't part of the conversation at all, it was as though he weren't even there. And being the middle child in the family, he did not want to be ignored any more than he already was.

"Look who's here," Josh said, elbowing Wally. There, way down at the end of the bleachers, sat Caroline and Beth, who had come to watch Eddie practice. The coach liked to have a cheering section during practice, he'd told his team. He said it got players used to the hooting and hollering that went on during a real game. In fact, the coach seemed to do enough hooting and hollering all on his own, Wally thought.

"Okay, players, look here!" Coach Malloy called out, holding up a glove. "When you catch a ball, catch it right here in the upper palm—not in the web of your glove."

Wally leaned back until his head rested on the riser behind him. The clouds were swirling across the sky, but the air was mild, as though spring had finally made it over the mountains. He was trying to figure out how far apart one cloud was from another. He imagined himself a giant, stepping from cloud to cloud, looking down on the earth below.

Josh elbowed him again. "Come on, Wally, pay attention," he said. "We're supposed to be cheering the team."

Wally sighed and slowly pulled himself up to a sitting position again. Far down the bleachers he could see that Caroline, too, had sprawled out on her back and was watching the clouds. *Who invented the ball, anyway?* Wally wondered. Football, basketball, baseball, softball, volleyball, kickball, dodge ball, tennis, golf, Ping-Pong . . . He always read what a great invention the wheel had been, but what about the ball? Who got the credit for that?

"Wally, are you watching or what?" Josh said.

"I'm watching! I'm watching!" Wally said with fake enthusiasm.

"*I'm* paying attention!" said Peter.

Wally snapped to and studied the field below. Now the coach was explaining how to field a ground ball. Wally yawned.

Out of the corner of his eye he saw Caroline crawling along the bleachers toward him. She got halfway between the place where Beth was sitting and the place where the Hatford boys were sitting, then motioned Wally to come over.

Wally considered it. If he did, he would probably get into trouble. If he didn't, she'd probably crawl all the way over and drop things down the back of his shirt. Somehow, though, even talking with Caroline Malloy seemed more interesting than sitting here waiting to cheer for someone.

"I'm going over and sit with Caroline for a while," Wally told his brothers.

"You're nuts!" said Josh. And then, "*No,* Peter! You stay here. We're supposed to be rooting for Jake."

Peter stayed put.

Wally stepped behind Josh and Peter and walked over to the middle of the bleachers, where Caroline was still crawling on her hands and knees.

"What are you, a dog?" he said.

"I'm bored," she told him.

"Me too," said Wally.

"That's probably because we're not very good at sports," Caroline said. "Dad says that people who are good in sports don't get bored with them. It's people like us who would rather be up on a stage who get bored during ball games."

"This isn't even a game, it's practice, and I don't want to be up on a stage, either," said Wally.

Caroline seemed to be thinking that over. "Then what *would* you rather be doing?" she asked.

Wally shrugged. "Nothing. I just like to think."

"*Every*one thinks all the time, Wally! You don't have to sit and do nothing in order to think!"

"Well, I have my best thoughts when I do," Wally answered.

Caroline leaned closer, until she was within a few inches of Wally's face. "What kind of thoughts do you have, Wally? I really want to know."

She sounded as though she meant it. Out on the field the coach was yelling, "Keep your bat as still as possible till you're ready to swing. Don't wave it back and forth."

Wally sighed. He was glad it wasn't him down there on the ball diamond getting yelled at over a stupid ball. "Well," he said finally. "Things like . . . like how it would feel to be a giant walking from cloud to cloud. Or . . . well, you know how, if you watch ants building an anthill and taking food inside and all that, they don't even know you're there. Right?"

"Right," said Caroline.

"If you put a stick in their way, they'll crawl over it or around it, but they don't know how it got there. They don't know that your shoe has a foot in it. They don't know anything about people or bridges or rockets or anything. All they know is their own little anthill." He looked at Caroline out of the corner of his eye to see if she was laughing at him.

But Caroline seemed absorbed in what he was saying, so Wally continued: "What if we're like ants to some huge creatures we can't even see? What if our world is like a small anthill and huge scientists are studying us under a microscope like germs or something?"

He looked directly at Caroline as he asked the question. He really wanted to know if anyone else ever had the same thoughts he did. Caroline seemed deep in concentration as she studied his face. "Did you know that your eyes have little brown specks in them?" she asked.

Wally let out his breath and tipped back his head. He should have known better than to tell anything like that to Caroline Malloy. But just when he'd decided she was hopeless, Caroline said, "I think about things like that too, sometimes."

"Like what?" asked Wally.

"Like what if every person who ever lived leaves a sort of ghost behind, and if conditions are absolutely exactly right, you can feel what that person was feeling when he died. For just a minute, maybe, you can sort of *be* that ghost."

"Like . . . like what do you mean?" asked Wally.

"Let's say that . . . well, that the baseball diamond was once a battlefield in the Civil War, and soldiers died right down there, and if either Eddie or Jake was standing in the exact spot in the exact position at the exact time on the exact day of the year that a soldier was killed, it would be as though Eddie or Jake was right there with him in the war."

That *was* an interesting thought, Wally decided. Of course, the odds of something like that happening would be one in a billion, which was why people didn't see ghosts more often than they did, but maybe it *could* happen. Maybe Caroline *was* precocious after all.

"And if you were that person standing where the soldier was killed," Caroline continued in a low, whispery voice, "you could feel what he felt when he died."

Wally squirmed a little. "You mean . . . if a bullet entered his brain . . ."

"Exactly. You would feel the white-hot blast in your right temple, and—"

"Never mind," said Wally. "I don't want to hear the rest."

"But then, when a minute was over, you would be yourself again, but you'd know exactly what it felt like to be a Civil War soldier and to be scared and shot."

"Grip the ball with your thumb on the bottom, Eddie," the coach was shouting, "not the side! Let's see that pitch again."

"Wally," said Caroline, "do you think we could ever be best friends?"

"Nope," said Wally.

"Why not?"

"It's like apples and oranges. We're too different."

"Because you're a boy and I'm a girl?"

"No, because you're . . . you're really weird sometimes."

"And you're not?"

"I'm just weird in a different way."

"Well, we could be friends even if we're not best friends, couldn't we?"

"I don't know," said Wally. "I'll think about it."

Nine

■

Letter to Georgia

Dear Bill (and Danny and Steve and Tony and Doug):

Now that we've got e-mail, you can get this letter about as fast as I can type it.

You want the Malloy girls? You can have the Malloy girls, especially Caroline. You know what she did now? She fell in the river. And you know how we got in trouble? Trying to save her, which we did, that's how!

It all started with the bottles. We each put a note in a bottle with our name and phone number on it and threw it in the river. Whichever one of us has a bottle that goes the farthest by April 30 gets to be King or Queen for a Day, and all the rest of us have to be servants.

But Caroline and her sisters were down at the river probably trying to fish our bottles out so they wouldn't go anywhere, and Caroline fell in. She was swept around the end of Island Avenue, so we ran to the other side with Beth and Eddie and made a human chain across the shallow part, and what do we get? Dad chews us out for being down at the river in the first place.

I think I could be happy without any more excitement. I could be happy to be a little bit bored now and then. I think I am very lucky not to have any sisters at all. What do you think?

Wally (and Jake and Josh and Peter)

■ ■ ■ ■ ■ ■ ■ ■ ■ ■ ■ ■

Ten

■

Letter from Georgia

Dear Wally (and Jake and Josh and Peter):

Yeah, e-mail rules! Except somebody e-mailed a love letter to a girl in my class and signed my name and now she hates my guts.

I don't want the Malloy girls. You can have them. I don't want any sisters or girlfriends, either. But I would sure like a little more excitement in my life than we've got here in Georgia.

I don't know if we're coming back or not. Mom and Dad keep saying things like "if we stay." I don't want to stay. I want to come back to West Virginia. I want to come back even if the Malloys stay and we have to live somewhere else.

Bill (and Danny and Steve and Tony and Doug)

P.S. Next time Caroline falls in the river, just wave good-bye.

Eleven

■

Contests

Caroline did not know why her father had to be so angry at her. They had *all* been down at the river, after all. She just happened to be the one who'd fallen in.

Didn't she get any points for not drowning? Didn't she get any credit for grabbing on to a floating tree limb and using it to hold herself up?

"And after I *told* them—I don't know how many times—to stay away from the river when it's high!" Mrs. Malloy had said, over and over again. "All they were going to do, they said, was have a bottle race. Caroline, what *possessed* you to get so close to the water?"

All Caroline could say under Eddie's stern gaze was that she had been trying to fish something out. She didn't say what. How could you tell your parents that you had made a deal with the Hatfords and were trying to cheat before they did?

But all the girls, not just Caroline, were grounded

for a week. Eddie was being punished because, as the oldest, she had not stopped her youngest sister from doing something dangerous, and Beth was being punished for going along with the others.

"School and baseball practice only," their father said. No bookstore, no playground, no drugstore, no library, and no friends invited to the house.

"At least they didn't say we couldn't talk to each other," said Caroline. "Now, that would have been unbearable."

"Oh, I don't know, Caroline," said Beth. "I think I could enjoy a whole week of reading uninterrupted."

"Yeah, I could enjoy a Caroline-free week, come to think of it," said Eddie, grinning at Beth.

Caroline flounced off, knowing in her heart of hearts that if she weren't around, her sisters' lives would not be half as interesting as they were.

■

The Friday after her scene in the river, however, Caroline found that *school* had become a lot more interesting, for Miss Applebaum announced that the county spelling championship would take place at the end of the month, right there in the auditorium of Buckman Elementary.

"This is why we have been working so hard on our vocabularies," she said. "This is why I've asked you to look for new words in the dictionary and include at least five new ones in every book report you write. It's why I've asked you to use a new word each night at the dinner table. For the next week I would like you to use a new word each time you ask a question in class, and if you can't see that word in your head—if you aren't sure how to spell it—then look it up and *make* sure."

Caroline promptly raised her hand. "Miss Applebaum, I surmise that our esteemed parents will be in close proximity when we congregate in the auditorium for our spelling bee?"

Wally turned and stared at Caroline with a look of disgust on his face, and some of the kids laughed, but Miss Applebaum was smiling. "Very good, Caroline! Yes, the countywide spelling bee will be held on the last Saturday of April, and of course parents are invited. For the very laws of our land are written in sentences, and sentences are composed of words, which *must* be spelled correctly if they are to mean anything at all."

"Do we *have* to take part in the spelling bee?" asked another girl.

"Let's try to use a new word in that sentence, Kimberly," Miss Applebaum said. "Can you ask that question another way?"

"Are you going to force us to be in the spelling contest?" Kimberly wanted to know.

"Every class in every school in the county will have its own spelling bee next Monday, and yes, I expect you to take part in that," Miss Applebaum said. A low moan traveled around the room. "But," the teacher continued, "only the top student in each class will be the finalist in the *county*wide spelling bee."

Caroline smiled smugly. She knew who number one would be. Her only possible rival might be Wally Hatford. He wasn't so good in math, and he was pretty horrible at music and art, but he could ace every spelling test that came along. She didn't know how he did it.

At lunchtime, when Wally was putting his books away, Caroline leaned over his shoulder and said, "Isn't this exciting, Wally? Wouldn't it be great if one of us was the finalist for our room?"

"No," said Wally.

"Why not?" said Caroline.

"Because it wouldn't," he said.

"Well, how come you're so good at spelling, then?" Caroline persisted.

"I don't know," said Wally, grabbing his lunch bag and heading for the all-purpose room.

Caroline ran after him and tugged at his sleeve. "Well, then, if you really don't want to do it, why don't you miss a word on purpose and let *me* win the spelling bee for our class?" And then, unable to stop herself, she said, "Let *me* be the reigning spelling-bee queen for Upshur County."

Wally stopped in his tracks. He turned and stared at Caroline as though he had never seen her before. As though she were a little bug he was examining under a microscope.

"Never!" he said, wheeling around again, and went off to eat at the boys' table.

Caroline sat down on a chair and took out her egg-salad sandwich. She would be queen of something yet. She just *had* to be!

■

"This is a weird school," Beth announced at dinner that evening. "It's spring, and somehow all these contests and tournaments are coming up. It's as though no one can do anything unless it's a game."

"What are you talking about?" asked her mother.

"First they've got baseball. You can't just divide up all the kids who want to play into two groups and let them play each other. You've got to have teams and play against other schools."

"So what's wrong with that?" said Eddie. "That's what sports are all about. I think it's great."

"Well, maybe for baseball it's okay, but now there's going to be a spelling contest in each class, and after that a countywide spelling bee, and then I suppose there will even be a national contest," Beth went on.

"I think it's rather nice," said Mrs. Malloy, taking a roll from the bread basket and reaching for the butter. "I think a spelling bee should be every bit as exciting as a baseball game."

"But now they're doing it to books!" Beth protested. "As soon as we got back from spring vacation, the principal promised that if the whole school read a thousand books by the end of April, he'd spend the night on the school roof."

Mr. Malloy laughed. "Why, that's a great idea! What better way to get kids into reading than for their principal to promise to do something ridiculous?" He laughed some more. "Boy, will he be miserable. He'd better hope it doesn't rain."

"Dad, listen to yourself!" Beth scolded. "The principal will do something ridiculous and miserable if we will do something miserable and ridiculous first?"

"Yeah, Dad," put in Eddie. "Read a thousand books and make yourselves miserable. Is that what he's saying?"

"You should read books because they're *fun*! Because you enjoy it!" said Caroline.

Mrs. Malloy looked at her husband and smiled. "They've got you there, George! The principal *is* sending the wrong message."

"He shouldn't have to send any message at all," said Beth. "It's like telling us that he'll spend the night on the roof if we'll eat a thousand hot fudge sundaes. It's something we want to do anyway. He doesn't have to bribe us."

Her father wiped his mouth with his napkin. "You know, it's times like this that make me feel I've got the wisest daughters in the world," he said. "And it's things like the three of you playing too close to the river that make me think you were born without brains. So, on balance, I'd say you're okay kids after all. But how does the principal know whether you really read a book or just said you did?"

"We have to write the titles on a chart, and the teacher asks us questions about the books to make sure we read them all the way through," Beth explained.

The telephone rang just then and Caroline, who was closest, picked it up and held it to her ear. "Hello?"

"Caroline?" said the voice. "This is Wally."

"Yes, Wally?" Caroline purred. "Have you decided to let me be the spelling-bee queen from our room?" She could hear her family groaning in the background.

"No," said Wally. "But I was wondering. Do you itch anywhere?"

"What?"

"I mean, are any of you scratching a lot, and do you have a rash on your stomach?"

"What?" Caroline shrieked.

"What's the matter?" asked her mother.

"It's Wally Hatford, and he wants to know if we itch."

"What?" yelled Beth and Eddie together. "Does he think we have fleas or something?"

"No, we don't itch," Caroline said into the telephone. "Why do you want to know?"

"Because if you do, you might have what Peter's got," Wally answered. "Chicken pox. Have a nice day!" And he hung up.

■ ■ ■ ■ ■ ■ ■ ■ ■ ■ ■ ■

Twelve

■

Go Directly to Jail

Peter sat miserably in his father's big chair in the Hatfords' living room, wrapped in a quilt, a thermometer in his mouth. He was listening to his mother make phone calls to the parents of all his friends, telling them that their child might be coming down with chicken pox too. Mrs. Hatford had asked Wally to call the Malloys.

There was something extremely satisfying, Wally discovered, in telling Caroline she might get chicken pox. He was still smiling when he hung up the phone. Three other kids in school had been sick with chicken pox in March. He imagined Caroline with red splotches on her face and arms, Caroline scratching her legs and stomach. He was glad *he* wasn't the youngest one in the family, having to stay home from school and scratch.

"I don't know what you're smiling about, Wally," said his mother as she slid the thermometer out of

Peter's mouth and checked it. "*You* haven't had chicken pox yet."

Wally stopped smiling. "You mean *I* could get it?"

"Yep. Three down, one to go," said his father. "Jake and Josh had it as babies. Let's hope you'll be next."

Wally stared at him in disbelief. They actually *wanted* him to get chicken pox? They actually *wanted* him to scratch and squirm? What kind of parents *were* these, anyway?

"It can be a lot more dangerous if you get chicken pox as an adult," his mother explained. "Go get Peter some orange juice, would you?"

Wally got the juice for Peter, being as careful as he could not to touch him. Then he went upstairs to the twins' bedroom, where his brothers were lying on their beds, each reading a mystery. Wally sat down at the foot of Jake's bed, his shoulders slumped.

Jake peered over the top of his book. "What's with *you*?"

"Life isn't fair," said Wally.

"You're just finding that out?" said Josh.

"And I don't want to be in that old spelling contest either," Wally continued.

"So don't! Misspell a word or something," said Jake. "That's simple. Eliminate yourself in the first round."

"I *can't*!" Wally said. "Caroline's going to be in it. And if Caroline wins, she'll be the most stuck-up, conceited know-it-all in the world. She even *asked* me to misspell a word so she could be the winner."

"Ha! She takes after her oldest sister," said Jake. "You know who's going to be the star of the baseball team, don't you? Eddie. I'll bet she gets to pitch every game, and she'll probably make the most home runs, too."

"And of course you know who's going to read the most books just to get the principal to spend the night on the roof," said Josh. "Beth, that's who."

"She'll probably read three books a week," said Jake.

"Ha! She'll read three books a day!" Josh told him.

"I thought you liked Beth," said Wally.

"Well, she's the nicest one of the three, but are we going to let them beat us at everything?" Josh said.

"I *told* you what would happen if the girls stuck around," said Jake. "The girls are taking over, that's what. You've *got* to be in that spelling contest, Wally, and you've got to win it for your grade."

"For the school," said Josh.

"For *us*! The Hatfords!" said Jake.

Wally threw back his head and howled in despair. "I know just what will happen! If I stay in the contest, Caroline and I will be the last two left, and I'll get chicken pox and Caroline will win."

"Naw," said Josh. "It takes at least two weeks for the spots to show up after you've been exposed. The school spelling contest is next Monday. You couldn't possibly get chicken pox by then."

"Unless he caught it from someone else and was already exposed," said Jake.

Wally fell back across the foot of Jake's bed, and all three boys lay staring up at the ceiling.

Finally Josh said, "I *thought* I wished they'd stay in Buckman, but now I'm not so sure. If Eddie wins at baseball and Beth wins at books and Caroline wins the spelling bee, where does that leave *us*?"

"Losers," said Jake.

Another minute passed in silence.

"There's only one thing that would be more horrible," said Wally at last.

"What?" asked Jake and Josh together.

"If Caroline's bottle traveled the farthest and she got to be Queen for a Day."

Jake and Josh sat up and looked at Wally. "You've *got* to win that spelling contest, no matter what!" said Josh.

■

Wally sat on the edge of the bed in his own room and wondered if he was beginning to itch. He pulled up his shirt and checked his stomach. No red spots. He rolled up the sleeves of his polo shirt and checked his arms. No red blotches there, either. Yet was his throat beginning to feel scratchy? Were his cheeks hot? He didn't dare get sick and let Caroline Malloy win the spelling bee.

He didn't know himself why he was such a good speller. Spelling just came easy to him. Maybe because he liked to look at things and study them. Even words. Even the letters that made up words. Whenever he heard a new word, it was as though he saw it on a billboard in his head. He liked looking up words in the dictionary to see how they were spelled. He liked taking them apart and putting them back together again. Which came first, the *i* or the *e*? The *h* or the *t*?

It was sort of like watching ants build an anthill, or a spider weave a web. He just liked to see how things were made, that was all. How stuff was put together. Words were just another kind of stuff. And almost always, when he got his spelling paper back, there was a big red 100 at the top, and often a comment from Miss Applebaum: *Good work, Wally!*

■

The one thing the boys were sure of, however—they had to stay on friendly terms with the girls. If they didn't, it might look as though they were jealous. As though they couldn't bear to let the girls be best at anything—and if ever there was a sore loser, it was someone who behaved like that.

So on Saturday, when it rained and the Malloy girls phoned and asked the boys if they wanted to come over and play Monopoly, the boys knew they had to go. Mrs. Hatford had taken the week off from her work at the hardware store to take care of Peter, and since Mrs. Malloy had assured Mrs. Hatford that all her girls had had chicken pox, Mrs. Hatford said, "By all means, *go!*" It was enough to have one sick boy in the house. She didn't want three more boys moping about the place.

They slogged across the bridge and up the rain-soaked hill to the Malloys' back door. Then, leaving their raincoats and wet sneakers in a pile, they trooped into the dining room, where Eddie had the board all set up and the money counted.

Wally sighed and slid into a chair. He didn't especially care for Monopoly, but it was better than sitting across from Peter and watching him scratch. But Wally was tired of chilly weather and rain and just wished summer would hurry and get there. That the Bensons would come back and life would settle down into the quiet, peaceful way it had seemed to be before the Malloys came to town. Well, maybe he didn't want it *too* quiet and peaceful. Maybe a *little* more exciting than when the Bensons lived there.

"What color marker do you want, Wally?" Beth was saying. "We lost the ones that came with the set. Do you want purple or black?"

"I'll take purple," chirped Caroline.

That left Wally with black. Of course, black! On a gray day in a gray rain under a gray sky, what could be more natural than black?

Jake tossed the dice first and the game began, the pieces moving slowly around the board—properties being sold, houses bought, hotels built.

Wally heard Coach Malloy come in. He heard the TV go on in the kitchen and a news program begin. He could hear the pans rattling as Mrs. Malloy started to bake something, the *chop, chop* of her knife on the cutting board.

Wally's piece landed on a space that told him to draw a card. He lifted one and turned it over.

Go directly to jail, the card said. *Do not pass Go.* Of course. What else could happen on a gray and rainy day?

At that moment, however, there was a knock at the front door. The three Malloy girls looked at each other in surprise because almost everyone came to the back door between the house and the garage.

"Can you get that, George?" Mrs. Malloy called, and there was the sound of Coach Malloy's footsteps in the hallway. Wally watched him pass the living room doorway and open the front door.

Everyone stopped playing Monopoly, for there stood a state trooper and Sergeant Bogdan from the police department, their badges gleaming from the light in the hall.

"George?" said Sergeant Bogdan. "This is Officer Leon Olson from state police headquarters. I need to tell you that we have a warrant to search your house." And he held out a paper for Coach Malloy to read.

"What?" said Coach Malloy as his wife came in from the kitchen.

"*Search* us?" said the girls' mother. "Why?"

In answer, the state trooper asked, "Does this house have a basement?"

"Yes," said the coach, pointing toward the cellar door off the kitchen.

"I'm real sorry about this, Coach," said Sergeant Bogdan, "but it's something we've got to do."

"But *why?*" said Mrs. Malloy again.

By now the Malloy girls had crowded into the hallway, the Hatford boys behind them, and it was obvious to Wally that nobody was going to explain anything until the basement had been searched.

Man! thought Wally. *This* was something that had never happened when the Bensons lived there. He couldn't ever remember the Bensons being searched. Maybe the Malloys were spies or something!

As the two policemen went down the basement stairs, Eddie said, "Can they just walk in people's homes like this, Dad, and search the place?"

"With a search warrant they can," her father said.

"But what would they be looking for?" Mrs. Malloy anxiously asked her husband. "We've done nothing wrong!"

There were sounds of things being moved around on the cement floor below. And finally there were footsteps on the stairs again, coming up. Then Sergeant Bogdan and the state trooper stood once again in the hallway.

"Jean and George, I'm real sorry about this intrusion, but it seems somebody found a note in a bottle and turned it over to the state police," the sergeant said. "Officer Olson here called me and asked me to check it out with him, so we did."

"A note in a bottle!" cried Mrs. Malloy. "The bottle race? This is crazy! What does it say?"

The trooper unfolded a small sheet of note paper

and read the message aloud: *"Help! This is no joke. I am being held prisoner in a cellar with hardly anything to eat. They beat me every day. Please call this number and ask for C. She'll tell you that what I say is true. Oh, please, please get me out before they kill me."* And the Malloys' phone number followed.

Thirteen

■

Jail

The trooper hadn't even said her name, yet everyone—her parents, her sisters, Sergeant Bogdan, the state trooper, and the three Hatford boys, their mouths hanging open in astonishment—was staring at Caroline. She could almost feel the color drain from her face, and knew she had done something awful. Yet the first words out of her mouth were "How far did the bottle go?"

"Caroline Lenore!" cried her mother. "Are you responsible for this?"

"It was . . . it was just . . . to make sure somebody called me if they found my bottle," Caroline said in a voice scarcely above a whisper.

Coach Malloy glared at all the kids in turn, as though ready to blame the lot of them.

"A woman found the bottle along the river just below Hall," the trooper said. "She called the state police from there."

Hall? Caroline thought in dismay. *That little place north of Buckman? That's as far as it got?*

"But why on earth would you write such a thing?" Mrs. Malloy asked incredulously. "You said it wasn't a joke, and it *was* a joke! Caroline, how could you *do* this?"

Caroline was crying now, really crying. She tried to imagine herself in a courtroom, facing a stern judge—how she would drop to her knees with her arms folded over her chest and throw herself on the mercy of the court. But the tears that were rolling down her cheeks now were real, because she realized that her parents were furious with her.

"Eddie!" boomed their father. "Do you know anything about this note?"

"I didn't know she was going to write a goofball letter like that! We were just going to write a little message about how important it was that somebody call us before the end of the month. We weren't supposed to write the script for a play!" Eddie said.

"Then why did you make up such a story?" Mrs. Malloy asked Caroline.

"I—I was afraid that if I d-didn't make it sound important, someone might find my b-bottle and not call," Caroline explained in a near whisper.

"And by that silly action you have wasted the time of a state trooper and the Buckman police department," said Coach Malloy.

"Not to mention the embarrassment this has caused our family!" said Caroline's mother.

"Were you boys in on this bottle race too?" Coach Malloy thundered, turning to the Hatfords.

"Yes, but—" Josh began.

"This isn't the first time we've been called over here either," said Sergeant Bogdan, "and it's always about something these kids have cooked up together."

"What do you think, Sergeant?" asked Coach Malloy. "What would be a proper punishment for Caroline? And I think all these kids should be included—the boys, too."

"What?" cried Wally.

"That's not for me to say," said Sergeant Bogdan.

But Beth was astonished. *"Us?"* she cried. "What did *we* do?"

"Since we've moved to Buckman, the authorities have been called out because Wally was trapped in the garage with a cougar, because a girl was missing after being lured over here to see an abaguchie, because you kids were playing around the river, because of a note in a bottle. . . . What am I missing? I'm sure there were others. You've taken up the valuable time of the police or fire department one too many times, *all* of you." Coach Malloy turned toward the policemen. "I'd like to volunteer these kids to do some work down at the police station, whatever you've got. And I'm sure that when I tell Tom Hatford what's happened now, he'll agree with me."

"You mean . . . like . . . *jail*?" Caroline gasped,

imagining herself in an orange prison jumpsuit with a number stamped on the back.

"He probably means cleaning *toilets*!" Wally proclaimed.

"Caroline, you knucklehead!" said Beth. "I don't want to clean toilets!"

"What time do you want them to show up for duty, Sergeant?" said Coach Malloy.

"Dad!" cried Eddie. "I've got baseball practice!"

"So do I!" said Jake. "It's not fair!"

"I didn't mean for this to happen," Caroline sobbed. "I didn't mean to get the other kids in trouble."

"Of course not! Not any more than falling in the river," her mother said.

Caroline looked desperately around the group, searching for a friendly face. "I throw myself on the mercy of the court," she said in a pitiful little voice.

"Go throw yourself in the river!" Jake muttered.

"She tried that already and it didn't work," Wally muttered back.

"Whenever you kids take up our time, whether you meant to do it or not, it's time we might have been called on to help someone in *real* trouble," said Sergeant Bogdan.

"They'll be at the police station tomorrow afternoon," said Coach Malloy. "I think two days of helping out around the place should do it."

"Well, we've got an inspection coming up the end of

the month, and the reception area could use some cleaning," said Sergeant Bogdan, warming to the idea. "It would be much appreciated." And then, with a wink at the girls' father, he said, "Nice of you kids to volunteer. See you tomorrow."

Caroline could hardly bear the disgust of the Hatford boys as they pulled on their soggy sneakers, picked up their raincoats, and stomped home. She closed her eyes against the disappointment of her parents, but it was the fury of her sisters she dreaded most, and they let her have it the minute they got upstairs.

"You idiot! Don't you *think* before you do something?" Eddie exploded. "Now we're all in trouble because of *you*!"

"I'm sorry," Caroline wept.

"Sorry doesn't help!" said Beth. "What did you *think* would happen when someone found that note? *This is not a joke,* you wrote. Of *course* they'd call the police. Of *course* the police would check it out."

Caroline went into her room, closed the door behind her, and crawled under the covers with all her clothes on. She didn't think she would ever come out again. She would go down in the *Guinness World Records* as the person who crawled into bed as a girl and stayed there for ninety years. Her hair would grow white and her nails long, and she'd lose all her teeth and they'd feed her through a straw, but she still wouldn't get out of bed. Then she had a thought: How would she go to the bathroom? Well, maybe she would get out of bed for that.

■

After the Hatford boys had come home from church on Sunday and both families had eaten their lunch, Caroline and her sisters set off. At the end of the footbridge the Hatford boys—all but Peter—were waiting, but they were not waiting for her. Beth and Eddie walked on ahead with Josh and Jake and Wally, and they all turned their backs on Caroline.

Caroline began to sing a song her grandmother used to sing:

> *"Lonely and friendless and poor,*
> *Nothing but sorrow I see,*
> *For I'm nobody's darlin',*
> *Nobody cares for me."*

She sang it softly at first, then more and more loudly, until the others up ahead could not help hearing her.

Eddie turned around. "*Can* it, Caroline!"

"Are you guys going to stay mad at me forever?" Caroline asked plaintively. "If we all hadn't sent bottles downstream, it wouldn't have happened."

"At least *your* bottle didn't go very far," Wally told her. "At least *you* won't be queen."

They walked down to the business district and into the police station. Sergeant Bogdan was talking to a new recruit. "Oh, yes. Here comes the Dirt Squad," he said when he saw Caroline and the others. "Officer Clay, these are the Hatfords and the Malloys, who live just up the river. Coach Malloy has asked if we could give them some cleanup jobs to do around here. Where do you think they should start?"

The new officer looked around. "Seems to me about every square inch of this place could use some work," he said, and Caroline's heart sank. Forever! That's how long she'd be here!

"Well, gang," said Sergeant Bogdan. "How about doing the rest room and the windows to begin? The broom closet's back there—you'll find the rags and the window cleaner. We'll consider this a practice run. Then I want you back here the last Saturday of the month to get the reception area ready for inspection. Nine o'clock sharp."

The kids quietly set to work. Anytime a look was directed at Caroline, she noticed, it was a scowl, not a smile. Wally purposely bumped into her every time he passed, Beth turned the other way, and Jake muttered, "Well, are you happy now?" as though she were the sole cause of their misfortune.

They put Caroline to work in the rest room, of course, while the others did the windows at ground level, inside and out. As she bent over the dirty toilet, holding the brush in both hands and scrubbing as hard as she could, Caroline muttered, "They want this place clean and beautiful, huh? Well, *I'll* give them beautiful. I'll make this place so beautiful they'll hardly know it's a police station."

And her lips began to curl at the corners with just a hint of a smile.

Fourteen

■

The Fatal Word

It was the day of the classroom spelling contest, and before Wally was fully awake, he found himself scratching all over. He scratched one arm, then the other, and then his stomach.

His eyes opened wide. No! It couldn't be. Not chicken pox! He *had* to go to school. He *had* to keep Caroline from winning the contest for their room.

He got out of bed and waited till everyone was out of the bathroom. Then he hurried inside and shut the door. In the mirror his face looked okay, though his ears were a little red. But when he took off his T-shirt and checked his arms and stomach, he saw the beginning of a faint red rash and knew without a doubt that he had chicken pox. He *hadn't* caught it from Peter. He must have been near someone else at school who wasn't showing a rash yet.

Even though the day was warm, Wally put on a long-sleeved shirt and buttoned it to the top. He waited till most of the others had eaten breakfast, then gulped down a glass of juice.

"Hey, Wally," Josh said as he packed his lunch at the counter. "Somebody must be talking about you. Your ears are red."

"Probably old Car-o-line," said Jake. "Figuring how she can get Wally to clean that toilet for her at the police station. Get us in even *more* trouble than we are."

Peter came into the kitchen just then. "Guess what, Wally?" he said. "My pox is almost gone. And guess what else? Mom thought maybe I could clean out my closet while I was home, but she didn't make me do it after all."

"Lucky you," said Wally. "When are you going back to school?"

"Soon, Mom says," Peter told him.

All the way to school, Wally lagged behind the others so that no one else would notice his ears. Not until he took off his jacket, that is, and took his seat in front of Caroline.

"Wal-ly," she whispered from behind. "You must have done something really, really embarrassing, because your ears are red."

Wally said nothing.

"You're not running a fever, are you?" Caroline continued.

Wally shook his head.

Caroline poked him in the back with her ruler. "You're not sick, are you, Wally?" she asked. And then, before he could answer, she said, "You don't have chicken pox, do you?"

Wally turned his head to one side. "Shut up," he whispered over his shoulder.

And she did. Wally was afraid that Caroline would raise her voice and tell the teacher that he should be home in bed, but sometimes even Caroline was known to do the right thing. Or perhaps she didn't want anyone to be angrier with her than Wally and his brothers were already.

Miss Applebaum's face looked like Christmas. There seemed to be nothing she liked as much as a good test or a pop quiz or a multiplication contest or a spelling bee.

"All right, class," she said. "This is the day we've all been waiting for!" Was she nuts? Wally thought. "This morning we will have a spelling contest in this room to see which of you gets to represent our class in the county contest. For months now we have been checking our spelling, learning new words, circling words in our readers, and increasing our vocabularies. Today we will find out who has been working the hardest."

Miss Applebaum was even wearing a new shirt for the occasion, Wally noticed, as the teacher went on: "I want you all to line up around the room—one long line, please. I'm going to read the words in the order that they appear on the standard list, so whatever word you get will be entirely by chance."

As everyone got into line, Wally felt a wild urge to scratch his neck, but he didn't dare. He chose a place by the doorway and slowly scraped his back against the door frame.

"Are you ready?" Miss Applebaum called from her desk. She sounded like the hostess on a game show.

"Ready," answered a few of the students, Caroline among them.

"Not ready," a few of the kids said, and the others laughed.

"All right, I'll start on my left. You will each get a different word. If you don't spell it correctly the first time, you are out of the contest and may take your seat."

Several students laughingly tried to slip into their seats before the contest even began, but the teacher made them get back in line.

"Now, take your time," Miss Applebaum said. "Listen carefully to the word. Try to visualize it in your mind. You may ask to have it repeated, and you may ask to have it used in a sentence. Here we go."

Wally itched all over. Even the bottoms of his feet itched. He wanted to scratch parts of his body he would never scratch in public.

The teacher turned to the large girl at the front of the line. "Okay, Emily, you seem to be first. The word is *squirrel.*"

The girl blinked. Then she took a deep breath, her arms straight down at her sides. "*S-q-u-e-r-r . . . ,*" she said.

A low gasp went around the room.

"I'm sorry, Emily, but *squirrel* has an *i* before the *r*'s, not an *e*," Miss Applebaum said, and, looking chagrined, Emily took her seat.

How easy it would be to misspell a word and be done with it, Wally thought. How comforting it would be to go back to his seat and, with everyone's attention on the people up front, scratch to his heart's content.

"Joanne, you're next," said Miss Applebaum. *"Obstruct."*

Each time the teacher said a new spelling word, Caroline whispered a soft "I know it!" even though it wasn't her turn. She made Wally sick.

"Would you use it in a sentence, please?" the girl named Joanne said.

"Certainly: It is against the law to obstruct justice."

Joanne cleared her throat. *"O-b-s-t-r-u-c-t."*

"That's correct. Go to the end of the line for your second turn," said Miss Applebaum. "Kenny, your word is *substantial*."

Kenny spelled his word correctly and took his place behind Joanne.

As the words went on, the line moved forward slowly. A student either took his place at the end or sat down. There were two students in front of Wally. His neck itched. His toes itched. Even his eyelids seemed to itch. When the two girls in front of him missed their words, Wally was next.

Miss Applebaum smiled at him. "Wally, your word is *anonymous*."

Anonymous? thought Wally. *How come one kid gets* squirrel *and I get* anonymous? When would he ever use a word like that? Still, he was sure he'd seen it on paper.

"Would you use it in a sentence, please?" he asked.

"Of course. The man who gave the donation wishes to remain anonymous."

The first and last parts were easy, Wally thought, but what was the letter in the middle? He closed his eyes and tried to see the word. *E?* he wondered, his head feverish. No, *e* wasn't right.

"*A-n-o-n . . . ,*"he began, "*y-m-o-u-s.*"

"Correct. You may go to the end of the line."

Wally didn't know whether he was glad or disappointed. He wanted so much to scratch. His head throbbed and his cheeks felt on fire. He went to the end of the line and stood against the bookcase this time. He rubbed his arm against the sharp corner of an encyclopedia.

Three more students took a turn, and then Caroline was next. She smiled at the teacher. Then she turned and smiled at the class. Wally couldn't stand it. It was as though she were onstage. As though she expected everyone to clap and throw roses at her if she got her word right, and how could she miss? She was Little Miss Perfect!

"Ready?" asked the teacher.

"Ready," said Caroline in her queen-of-the-world voice.

Miss Applebaum looked at the list before her. "Your word is *precocious.*"

Wally closed his eyes. He knew it. Of course

Caroline would get a word like that. Of course she would get it right. Miss Applebaum might as well have asked her to spell her own name. He opened his eyes.

Caroline was so confident that she did not ask to have the word repeated. She did not ask to have it used in a sentence. She smiled again at the teacher. Smiled at the class. Then she opened her mouth and said, "*P-r-e-c-o-s-i-o-u-s.*"

Wally snapped to attention. It was wrong! She had spelled it wrong! Caroline Malloy's first word in the spelling contest, and she'd blown it!

And just as suddenly, Caroline, too, realized that she had it wrong.

"*C,*" she cried. "I meant *p-r-e-c-o-c-i-o-u-s!*"

Miss Applebaum looked at her sadly.

"Miss Applebaum, I knew that word! I knew it all along!" Caroline gasped. "I was just so excited that I got a word I knew that I spelled it too fast. It's *p-r-e*—"

"I'm sorry, Caroline, but the rule is that you have to spell it right the first time."

Caroline stared at the teacher without moving. Then she faced the class. "But I *knew* it!" she wailed. "I knew it, I knew it!"

"Sit down," somebody said.

"But I knew it!" Caroline kept repeating, tears forming in her eyes.

"Take your seat, Caroline," Miss Applebaum said.

The next girl correctly spelled *sergeant,* accompanied by soft wails from Caroline in the second row.

Wally stuck it out to the end. He correctly spelled

abruptly and *beneficial,* and then he was the last one left.

"Class, let's have a big round of applause for our fourth-grade winner," said Miss Applebaum. "Wally Hatford will go to the county spelling contest for our grade."

Everyone clapped. All but Caroline. She had her face buried in her arms, and every now and then her shoulders gave a little shudder.

Wally raised his hand. "May I go to the rest room?" he asked.

"Of course," said the teacher.

Wally walked stiffly from the room, feeling really sick. He went down the hall to the boys' rest room and shut himself in a stall. Then he scratched and he scratched and he scratched.

Fifteen

■

Clean and Beautiful

When the going gets tough, the tough get going.

That was what Coach Malloy would tell his football team when they were behind in a game. It hung on a plaque in the Malloys' kitchen, and now, the day after the school spelling contest, Caroline was looking up at it on the wall.

Maybe that was meant for her. The going had certainly been tough for *her* lately. It wasn't enough that she had fallen in the river and almost been swept away. Not enough that everyone was mad at her because of the note she had put in her bottle. Now she had blown the spelling bee as well, and it was Wally Hatford, not she, who would represent their fourth grade in the county contest. What a lousy April!

What she felt worst about, however, was that Beth and Eddie were hardly talking to her. Caroline couldn't bear being ignored. The next day after school, when the Hatford boys had gone on home, leaving the Malloy girls to walk alone, Caroline trailed woefully behind her sisters, who acted as though she weren't there.

Finally she said in a small sad voice, "So what am I? Just another leg, trailing along behind you?"

And when neither of them answered, she said, "Maybe I'm not even a leg. Maybe I'm just a foot. A tired old foot that just clumps along at the end of a leg behind her sisters."

Even though her sisters were ahead of her, Caroline could tell from the way their cheeks puffed out at the sides that they were smiling.

"A *shoe*!" Caroline cried pitifully. "A dirty old shoe with a floppy sole that—"

"Okay, okay," Eddie said, turning around and laughing. "Come on up and walk with us, but can you possibly stay out of trouble for once?"

"I never *tried* to get us in trouble," Caroline said. "I never *meant* for us to have to do work at the police station."

"That doesn't help," Eddie told her.

"Well, I'm sorry I got you guys mixed up in it. But it just might turn out to be fun."

"*Fun!*" cried Beth. "Are you crazy?"

"I've got an idea," Caroline confided.

"See?" said Eddie. "She's at it already."

"But this wouldn't hurt anyone," Caroline insisted.

"Okay. What?" Eddie asked.

"Well, you know how Sergeant Bogdan says he wants the station clean and beautiful the day of the inspection?"

"I heard the word *clean,* Caroline. I didn't hear the word *beautiful,*" Eddie told her.

"Okay, okay, so I made that part up," said Caroline. "But do you remember what we did to the Benson boys' rooms when they were here last month to visit?"

Eddie's eyes began to crinkle just a little at the corners. Beth's, however, opened wide.

"You don't mean . . . ?" Beth said, staring first at Caroline, then at her older sister.

"Not wallpaper or anything, but what if we . . . sort of . . . tied bows to the rolls of toilet paper, and put lace doilies on the tables in the reception room, and daisies on the sergeant's desk. Wouldn't that be a hoot?"

"They couldn't say we were doing any harm," Eddie agreed.

"And everything would be neat and clean," said Beth.

The girls looked at each other. "Let's do it!" they said.

"Just for the fun of it," said Eddie. "But I've got an even better idea. Let's don't tell the boys. Let's tell Sergeant Bogdan that Jake's in charge of the Dirt Squad, and to let him assign us our jobs. Then, when all the stuff we've left behind is discovered, it's Jake who will get in trouble."

Beth clapped her hands gleefully.

"Except, of course, Jake will give us all the worst jobs to do," said Caroline.

"It'll be worth it," said Eddie.

■

Instead of going home—Mother was at a meeting of the Faculty Wives' Club, anyway—the girls knocked on the Hatfords' door. Jake answered. When he saw Caroline, he almost closed the door on her, but Eddie stopped him.

"Yeah?" he said.

"We just dropped by to say hello to Wally and see how he's doing," Eddie said.

"Well, he's . . . uh . . . ." Jake turned toward the living room and didn't seem to know how to answer.

But Peter, who had followed his older brother to the door, chirped, "He's right over there on the couch. But Mom made a cake for him because he's the spelling champion, aren't you, Wally?"

When the girls walked into the living room, they found Wally Hatford in his racing-car pajamas, with red spots all over his face and arms. He had just started to stand up and make his getaway, but it was too late. He sank back against the cushions and held a pillow in front of him to hide his pj's, and Caroline felt a sudden rush of pity for him. She really, truly did.

"How are you feeling, Wally?" she asked.

"How do you *think*?" he answered.

"Did you bring him anything?" asked Peter, studying

their pockets and backpacks, as though the girls might have a treat that Wally could share with his brothers.

"Just our cheerful faces," said Beth. "Congratulations on the spelling contest, Wally."

"Yeah, that must have been a big surprise for you, huh, Caroline?" Jake said with a smirk.

Wally wasn't smiling, however. He looked about as miserable as a person could look.

"We just came by to tell you guys that we're really sorry Caroline got you in trouble along with us, and we feel sort of responsible," Eddie said. "There isn't any way to make it up to you, I guess, but we'll let you be in charge of the Dirt Squad, as Sergeant Bogdan calls it, when we go to the police station at the end of the month. Just tell us what to do and we'll do it."

"Huh?" said Josh.

"We'll tell Sergeant Bogdan that we're taking our orders from you, Jake, and you can supervise," said Eddie.

Jake and Josh looked at each other quizzically.

"Because," said Beth, "if we do a really good job for them, maybe the police won't be so mad at us either."

"There are sure a lot of things happening at the end of April!" said Caroline. "The police station is being inspected, the principal spends the night on the roof if we read a thousand books, there's the county spelling contest, and one of us will win the bottle race."

"Well, *your* bottle won't make it, Caroline. It hardly went any distance at all," said Wally, and even his words sounded feverish.

"Unless nobody else's bottle is found," Caroline said.

The boys looked at each other uneasily.

"Anyway," Eddie said hurriedly, "Caroline is really sorry for all the trouble she's caused"—she paused and looked in Caroline's direction, and Caroline put on her most apologetic face—"and, with the baseball games starting next month, we just wanted to begin the season on good terms with everybody."

"Okay, if that's the way you want it," said Jake.

"Good," said Eddie. "Get well soon, Wally."

"Drink a lot of water," said Beth.

"And try not to scratch," said Caroline.

Sixteen

■

Bad and Worse

"They're up to something; you can count on it," said Josh.

"Caroline looked like the cat that swallowed the canary," said Wally.

"They must have been out of their minds," Jake gloated. "We'll give them the dirtiest jobs of all. I'll make them sorry they ever thought of making us boss."

"I think the girls are nice!" said Peter, settling down in his corner of the couch with a bag of pretzels. "I think they said nice things and you're just being mean to them."

"*Us?* Mean to *them?*" said Jake. "Peter, if Caroline hadn't written that stupid note, we wouldn't even have to do any work at the police station at all!"

"Well, I'll help," Peter offered.

"Fine. You can come too. We'll all be boss," Jake told him.

"Who was that?" Mrs. Hatford called from the kitchen, where she was making a pot of chicken soup for Wally.

"Just Caroline and her sisters, saying they're sorry," said Peter.

Mrs. Hatford came to the kitchen doorway. "Really? Maybe there's hope for that girl yet!" she said.

■

There was baseball practice every day after school, and by the following Monday Wally felt well enough to go watch Jake out on the ball diamond. Peter crawled up on the bleachers beside him and Josh.

"If we work hard at the police station, will it keep you from going to jail?" Peter asked.

"We're not going to jail," Josh said. "But Jake is really going to make the girls work!"

"No matter how hard he is on them, they'll be twice as hard on us if any of their bottles wins the race," said Wally.

"Whose bottle is ahead?" asked Peter.

"Caroline's is the only one that's been found so far. Boy, *some*body's bottle had better go farther than hers by April thirtieth."

Down on the field Eddie was up at bat, Jake pitching. The coach had divided the players in half, so that some were practicing batting and some were practicing fielding. Wally watched as the guys in the outfield automatically moved a few yards back whenever Eddie came up to bat. She even held the bat down close to the knob in a power grip, while a lot of the boys held the bat farther up for more control.

Whack! went the bat, and the boy in right field had to chase the ball along the ground before he could throw it back. By that time Eddie had made it all the way to third.

It was unsettling watching her play almost better than anyone else on the team. Jake had thought that he and Eddie were evenly matched, but if Wally had to bet on one of them, it would probably be Eddie.

During a break in practice Jake climbed up on the bleachers with a cup of Gatorade and sat down beside his brothers.

"Man, that Eddie is really good," Wally said.

"Yeah, *tell* me about it," Jake said sullenly. "Do you see how everyone moves back when she steps up to bat? Like she's the star! The big shot! Everybody will come to the game just to see Eddie Malloy play!"

"If anyone hears you talk like that, Jake, it'll sound like you're jealous," Josh said.

"Well, heck! Who wouldn't be? I've been waiting to get on the sixth-grade team since I was in kindergarten; waiting for when I could finally play for the Buckman Badgers. And now that I'm in sixth grade, what happens? Number one: our best friends move to Georgia; number two: the Malloys come to town; number three: we get in more trouble than we've ever been in before; and number four: Eddie Malloy makes the team big-time."

"So what can you do about it?" said Josh. "Nothing."

But Jake smiled just a little. "Not exactly. I'll work her like she's never been worked before at the police station. She won't be such a big shot then. She's really going to be sorry she made me boss."

The next practice day went even worse for Jake. He didn't get to pitch at all. The coach used Eddie as pitcher the whole time because she was so good at throwing strikes. It was as though Jake weren't even there.

And as if that weren't enough, when Jake got up to bat, Eddie struck him out. Not once, but twice. The ball came at him so fast he could hardly blink. What was she, a robot? A creature from outer space? Where had she learned to pitch like that? From her dad, of course, Jake grumbled to Wally.

Dinner that evening was especially miserable. No matter what dish Mrs. Hatford passed to Jake, he said it smelled rotten. It tasted awful. He wouldn't eat garbage.

"How about if you eat in your room for a week and get only bread and water?" Mr. Hatford said finally. "What's wrong with you, anyway? You're making the whole family upset."

"He's mad at Eddie," Peter volunteered, and Wally elbowed him.

"Pipe down," muttered Jake.

"Now, what could a girl do to put you in such a foul mood, Jake?" asked his mother.

"She struck him out two times!" said Peter.

"Ah!" said Mr. Hatford. "So that's it."

"Well, what do you expect? Her dad's a coach," said Jake. "Why couldn't *you* have been a coach, Dad, instead of a mail carrier?"

"Well, son," said his father, "that's the way the ball bounces. And your going around mad at Eddie Malloy isn't going to make you a better player. Maybe if you'd pay attention to the way she pitches and the way she swings, you'd learn a little something."

"Oh, I'm not really mad at her, I just hate her guts, that's all," said Jake. And he angrily attacked his scalloped potatoes.

■

Wally was never too good at sports himself, but he knew what it felt like to be jealous of someone. To feel that life was against you. To feel as though you'd like to catch the first bus out of town and never come back.

Josh wasn't much help because he was working on maps for geography, and when Josh made a map, it wasn't just the basic stuff; he put in mountains and rivers and all kinds of things the teacher hadn't required, just because he was so good at drawing. He only half listened to Jake's complaints.

It was Wally who sat on the sofa beside Jake after dinner and tried to think of something to cheer him up.

"She could always get sick before a big game, and then you'd pitch the whole time," Wally said.

"Eddie never gets sick. She's as strong as a horse. She's made out of steel or something," said Jake.

"She could trip sometime running bases and break her ankle," said Wally.

"Get real," said Jake.

The phone rang just then and Wally answered.

"If it's Eddie, I don't want to talk to her," said Jake.

"Hello?" said Wally.

"Is this the home of Jake Hatford?" asked a man's voice.

Wally hesitated. Was this more bad news or what? What had Jake done now?

"Yes," he said finally.

"Well, I thought he'd like to hear I found a bottle with his name in it, and I'm just calling to let him know," the man said pleasantly.

"Oh! Just a minute!" said Wally. "Jake! Someone found your bottle! Take the phone!"

Jake leaped up from the couch, tripping on his sneakers on the rug, and grabbed the phone.

"Hello?" he said. "Yeah . . . ? Yeah . . . ? Where did you find it?"

There was a long silence. Wally watched his brother, hoping for any piece of good news that might make him feel better. If one of their bottles could get past Hall at least, then Caroline wouldn't be queen.

"Oh," Jake was saying. Then, "Thanks a lot." He hung up.

"What did he say?" Wally asked. "Where did he find it?"

"It was stuck in the roots of a tree, and he found it when he went fishing," Jake said.

"But where?"

"Just under the road bridge to the business district," said Jake. He clomped upstairs, went into his room, and slammed the door.

Well, at least he didn't lie about it, Wally thought. He *could* have said the man found it in Cincinnati. But scarcely had the thought entered his mind when Jake came running down the stairs again.

"Hey, Wally, just forget I said that, huh? It wasn't the business district at all. It was over by the Ohio River."

"Jake, it was not. You're lying," Wally told him.

"What do *you* care? Do you want one of the girls to boss us around for a day?"

"I'm not lying for you, and that's that," said Wally.

"You don't have to lie. Just keep your mouth shut," said Jake.

"I won't do that either, and besides, it would never work," Wally told him.

"Why not?"

"Because you didn't ask the man what else was in the bottle. And if you can't name the secret thing the girls put inside it, it doesn't count."

Jake clutched at his head, moaned, kicked a chair, and for the second time went upstairs and slammed the door.

And Wally thought of another rule they'd have to add to the list: Whenever somebody got a phone call saying a bottle had been found, that person had to get a phone number for the caller, so that the others could check up on it. This was getting complicated!

Seventeen

■

Inspection

When Caroline and her sisters got to school the following Monday and walked inside, there was a huge banner in the hall above the doors to the auditorium: BUCKMAN ELEMENTARY HAS READ 1000 BOOKS!!!

On a large sheet of computer paper taped to the wall beneath were the names of all the students who had read a book in the past month, along with the titles each had read. Beth's name, of course, was at the very top, with the highest number: thirteen.

"Yeah, Beth! Way to go!" Eddie told her. "The girls are taking over!"

"What do you think, Wally?" Caroline said when she got to her room. "Are the Malloys good, or are we *good*?"

Wally only groaned. He didn't even turn around.

After "The Star-Spangled Banner" had been played over the classroom speakers and the Pledge of

Allegiance had been said, the principal's voice was heard: "Congratulations, Buckman students! Over one thousand books! I knew you could do it! And you reached our goal a week early! That means that when April is over, you will have read even more than a thousand books!"

Everybody clapped, and Caroline could hear the applause traveling up and down the hall from other classrooms. The principal went on: "I've been looking over the slips you've turned in, with the names of the books you've read. I see mystery, adventure, humor, and suspense. You've read historical books and nonfiction books and poetry and science fiction. I hope you have been introduced to whole new worlds—new places to explore—and that this will lead to a lifetime of reading enjoyment.

"And now I know you are all wondering when I will spend the night on the roof. It's already on my calendar, folks! Since the county spelling bee is going to be held the evening of Saturday, April twenty-eighth, I will be up on the roof on April twenty-ninth, rain or shine. I'll bring my tent and sleeping bag and, of course, a flashlight and a favorite book to keep me company. And when you come to school the next day, you can stand out on the playground and watch me eat my bowl of Wheaties in my pajamas."

Everyone laughed.

"So congratulations again, and especially to our very top winner, with thirteen books to her credit for the month—fifth grader Beth Malloy!"

There was more applause, and Caroline whispered, "What do you think, Wally? Aren't we great?"

But before Wally could answer, the principal went on: "I am *especially* proud of our school this spring—the thousand books, the Buckman Badgers, and all the wonderful winners of our school spelling bee who will participate in the county contest." Here he read off the winner in each classroom. When he came to Wally's name, everyone in Miss Applebaum's class clapped and cheered, and Caroline didn't poke Wally in the back this time. She even forced herself to clap too. Anyone who had looked as miserable with chicken pox as Wally had, she decided, deserved some applause.

When all the announcements were over, however, and the teacher was collecting lunch money, everyone began talking about the principal and whether or not he would actually spend the night on the roof.

"Do you think he'll really stay up there the whole night?" someone asked.

"I'll bet if it rains he won't," answered Caroline.

Wally turned around. "I'll bet he goes up there around seven with everyone watching, and about midnight he goes home and sleeps in his own bed."

"Well, I hope there's a thunderstorm and hail," a girl said.

"A tornado!" said somebody else, and everyone laughed.

Caroline leaned forward till her mouth was right

next to Wally's ear. "You know what might be fun to do, Wally? The Hatfords and the Malloys together? We could sneak over to the school about midnight and see if he's there."

And Wally whispered back, "Maybe we will."

At nine o'clock in the morning on the last Saturday of the month, the Hatford boys and the Malloy girls met at the police station, and Jake told Sergeant Bogdan that the girls had put him in charge of the Dirt Squad; he would make sure that everyone did a good job, and the place would be in top shape for the inspection.

"Good!" the sergeant said. "We're expecting Chief Decker at noon." He led Jake around the reception area, the others tagging along. "See this tile floor? It's been mopped, but it hasn't been scrubbed, really scrubbed, for years. I want this floor to gleam—every square inch of it. That'll mean getting down on your hands and knees with scrub brushes, poking in all the corners. The rest room needs cleaning again, the front window needs washing, and all the chairs along the wall over there need to be wiped down. . . . The little room we use for a kitchen needs a good cleaning—the microwave, the small fridge, the sink . . ."

He handed a list to Jake—all the work to be done from the front door of the station right back to the door to the holding cells—and when he'd returned to his desk, Jake faced the others. "Okay. Josh, you and I will do the chairs and window. Wally, you and Peter sweep the sidewalk out front and wipe off all the doorknobs. Eddie and Beth will get down on their hands and knees and scrub the floor, and Caroline will clean the rest room again, paying special attention to the toilet. When you're through with the floor, Eddie, do the kitchen."

Caroline could hardly stand it. "Wally does doorknobs and I do the toilet again?" she whimpered.

"It was you who got us into this, so you get the elephant's share," said Jake without pity.

"This floor is disgusting," Beth said after the boys had scattered to do their jobs. "There's even chewing gum stuck to it in places."

"Don't worry," Eddie told her. "It'll be worth it." She winked.

"You don't think we'll get in trouble over this?" Beth asked.

"Why would we?" Eddie grinned. "Jake's in charge, remember?"

Jake came by with the Windex. "What's so funny?" he asked.

"We're just telling jokes to make the time go faster," Eddie said.

"Well, don't forget to do the corners," he instructed.

"Yes, *sir*!" Eddie said, and gave a mock salute.

■

Forty-five minutes later, Sergeant Bogdan came down the hall. "Well, well, you make a good taskmaster, Jake, because I never saw this floor looking so good," he said.

"Thanks," Jake said.

Eddie gave a snort under her breath, but Bogdan didn't hear her.

About eleven that morning the girls were just putting away their mops and brushes when Sergeant Bogdan gave a little whistle.

"Son of a gun!" Caroline heard him say. "There's the inspector pulling up right now. He's early!" While he and the Hatford boys lined up outside to greet the police chief, the girls rushed about putting the final touches on the reception area. They heard Sergeant Bogdan say, "Chief Decker, I want you to meet Jake here. I've got a bunch of kids doing some . . . uh . . . volunteer work, you might say, sprucing up the station, and Jake Hatford's the guy in charge."

Caroline watched the man in the chief's uniform hold out his hand. "Glad to meet you," he said. "Maybe you'll go into police work one of these days yourself, young man. We need all the good men we can get. So you were in charge of the work detail, huh?"

"Yes, sir!" said Jake, his chest thrust out like he'd just won a gold medal or something.

"Well," said the captain. "Let's take a look around." They all came inside, and the captain just smiled at the girls who squeezed by them there in the hall.

"We're done," Eddie whispered to Jake.

"Yeah, see you later," said Beth.

"Have a nice day!" said Caroline as the girls went out the door.

Eighteen

■

The Decorators

Well, that *was a change,* Wally thought. He'd expected the girls, Caroline in particular, to hang around and claim the glory. He'd sort of expected *her* to say she had worked her fingers to the bone. She might even have pretended to faint from exhaustion.

Chief Decker, followed by Sergeant Bogdan, followed by Officer Clay, followed by the four Hatford boys, moved down the hall toward the little kitchenette behind the office. Everything was crisp looking and white, including a tall chef's hat with a pink ruffle around the bottom sitting on top of the microwave.

Wally stared at the ruffle while Jake and Josh stood with open mouths, speechless.

"Hey, look at the hippo!" Peter cried delightedly, pointing to a refrigerator magnet of a hippo wearing a pink tutu and eating a pizza.

Chief Decker turned slowly around the little kitchen. Pink curtains had been tacked over the small window above the sink, and a paper cup filled with daisies stood in the middle of the little table.

Without a word he moved on down the hall to the waiting room, and Wally sucked in his breath, because someone had put lace doilies over the backs of the vinyl chairs and tied bows at the bottom of each metal leg.

"Peppermints!" Peter cried, pointing to the dish of pink-and-white candies on the metal table beside the vinyl couch. On top of the TV, on another lace doily, a dime-store ballerina did a pirouette.

"Is this a police station or my aunt Millie's parlor?" asked Chief Decker with a frown, looking at the dazed faces of Sergeant Bogdan and Officer Clay.

The tile floor gleamed, the walls were spotless, the windows shining, but these were hardly noticed, for when they got to the rest room with its roll of toilet paper tied with pink ribbon, a pink ruffle taped around the lid of the toilet tank, plus a box of pink tissues by the sink and little stick-on hearts around the rim of the mirror, Sergeant Bogdan exploded.

"Jake, what the blazes were you kids trying to do? Embarrass us?" he asked, ripping off the pink ruffle and stuffing it in his pocket.

"We . . . I . . . the g-girls must have done this before they left!" Jake croaked.

"A good officer knows what his troops are doing," said Chief Decker, his eyes twinkling, "and he has to take full responsibility for his subordinates."

But the worst was yet to come, Wally discovered.

Because when they moved back out into the hall and looked in the other direction, toward the holding cells, they found that someone, and Wally knew who, had pasted on the wall row after row of round yellow smiley faces, now grinning at the police chief.

Wally couldn't tell whether Chief Decker was choking or coughing or laughing, and he didn't stick around to find out. All he knew was that he was racing down the hall after his brothers—out the front door of the station, down the steps, and then, as fast as they could go, toward home.

But a block away, the girls were waiting for them. Caroline and her sisters were leaning against a tree, helpless with laughter.

"You dumbos!" Jake yelled when he saw them.

"Oh, come on, Jake. You know it was funny," said Beth.

"Yeah, what are you going to do? Fire us?" Eddie teased.

"I thought the hippo in the pink tutu was the best," said Caroline. "Sergeant Bogdan can keep it if he wants, sort of a reminder of what he's going to look like if he keeps on eating so many doughnuts."

"Well, you could at least have let us in on the joke," Jake complained as they started home together. "I didn't know what to say. Bogdan kept looking at me as though—" He stopped suddenly. "That's why you put me in charge, isn't it?"

"Clever boy! You figured that out in a hurry," said Eddie. "Well, you worked us to death with all that scrubbing, so we earned the right to a little fun. I'd say we're about even."

"I thought it looked nice!" said Peter. "The peppermints were good too!" He held out his hand and showed them a fistful.

"See?" said Beth, laughing some more. "At least somebody appreciates all our work."

"I'd appreciate you a whole lot more if you'd just leave Buckman!" Jake growled.

"You'd miss us. You know you would," Beth cooed, and Wally noticed that Josh was even smiling a little.

Nineteen

■

Not Again!

Mrs. Malloy insisted that the whole family attend the countywide spelling contest that night, even though none of her daughters would be in it. "It's important to show our support for the language arts, just as much as it is to support the band concerts and ball games," she said.

"Why should I want to go see Wally Hatford win for the fourth grade?" Caroline whined. "*I* should be up there onstage, not Wally."

"Caroline, you missed your word, so you should *not* be up there," said her mother. "Those were the rules. Thinking things through and taking your time are important too, and you didn't do either of those. Now put on a clean shirt, and let's try to be at the school by seven so we don't have to sit at the very back."

It was almost more than Caroline could bear. It was like being a famous actress and having to sit in the audience while an understudy went onstage, playing your role. Wally Hatford was a good speller but he didn't like being in contests. He never even liked standing up in front of the room. Caroline *deserved* to be in that contest. She, who loved the stage and the spotlight, *deserved* to win for Buckman's fourth grade. She would have been so good at it. She could have worn her best dress, and she would have bowed to the audience when she won first place.

She changed her shirt, and out the door they went, crossing the swinging bridge on a beautiful April night, and walked two blocks to the school. Cars were lined up on each side the street, for people had driven in from all over the county. The air was filled with the sounds of friends calling to friends, parents calling greetings to parents, and contestants laughing and chattering.

The Malloys took seats in the middle of the auditorium and, after they sat down, discovered that the Hatfords—all but Wally, of course—were sitting in the same row across the aisle. Mrs. Malloy leaned forward and smiled, and Mrs. Hatford waved back.

The contest began about fifteen minutes later, with a great deal of lining up and changing places and counting heads before the contestants took their places in the first three rows of the auditorium. The winning first graders from all the schools went up onstage first.

When students spelled their words correctly, they went to the end of the line to wait for another turn. But if they missed, a teacher escorted them to the steps at one side of the stage, and they joined their classmates below.

The winning word for the first grade was *untie,* and everyone clapped as the boy who won it grinned and waved at his parents.

The second graders came onstage next, their arms straight down at their sides, looking even more serious. When only two girls were left onstage, one misspelled the word *dinosaur* and—to her even greater embarrassment—broke into tears and left the stage weeping.

The winning word in third grade was *discipline,* and then it was the fourth grade's turn.

"Remember," said the county superintendent, who was calling out the words. "You may ask to have a word repeated, and you may ask to have it used in a sentence." He also reminded the contestants that the winner for each grade would go to the statewide spelling contest in Charleston in May.

Miserably, Caroline watched as Wally Hatford shuffled across the stage, hands in his pockets, beside the other contestants. Mrs. Malloy leaned forward again and smiled down the row at Mrs. Hatford, and Mrs. Hatford leaned forward and smiled back.

"*Tremendous,*" said the superintendent to the first person in line. The girl spelled the word correctly and moved to the end.

"*Scissors,*" said the superintendent. The next girl mistakenly put an *e* before the *r* and was escorted offstage.

Wally was given the word *knowledge,* which he spelled correctly, and again the Malloys and the

Hatfords exchanged smiles. Peter clapped for his brother.

Caroline was silently weeping already. No actress should have to go through the agony she endured. *Look at Wally up there!* she thought. His shoulders were slumped, his eyes were on the floor, hands in his pockets, toes pointing inward. He looked as uncomfortable and awkward as an elephant at a tea party. Wally no more wanted to go to the state contest than he wanted to go to the dentist. *She* would have been such a wonderful contestant to represent Buckman's fourth grade! She would have gone on to the state contest, and then the national, and she would have been on TV. From there it was only a short step to Broadway. Oh, life was so unfair!

One more contestant was eliminated as the line moved toward the superintendent, and once again it was Wally's turn.

"*Handkerchief,*" said the superintendent.

Oh, that's so easy! Caroline thought. That was the easiest word so far! She could spell much harder words than that.

"*Handkerchief,*" Wally repeated, looking straight ahead. "*H-a-n-d . . .*" He hesitated, and Caroline knew with every bone in her body that he was about to misspell it so that he wouldn't have to go to the state contest. He would probably put in a *c* instead of a *k*.

"Uh . . . ," said Wally.

"I know it!" Caroline cried, suddenly leaping to her feet.

"Caroline!" whispered her mother.

"*H-a-n-d-k-e-r-c-h-i-e-f!* I'm from Buckman Elementary too! I'm in fourth grade too, and I *know* it!" she pleaded while people in front turned to stare at her and her mother frantically lunged across Eddie's lap, trying to grab her arm.

Impulsively Caroline whirled and faced the audience. "But I *know* it!" she cried, sure that *someone* would see the justice of her taking Wally's place. Instead of a sea of smiling faces, however, Caroline saw only disgust and ridicule. She turned slowly around again.

"Will the young lady in the pink shirt please sit down?" said the superintendent, unsmiling.

Caroline tearfully collapsed on her seat, her face beet red with embarrassment. Beth and Eddie had their hands over their faces, Coach Malloy was glaring down the row at her, and up onstage, Wally's face was as pink as Caroline's shirt.

"We'll try you on another word, son," the superintendent said. He turned to look at Caroline again and said, "I trust there will be no more outbursts."

Eddie clapped her hands over Caroline's mouth. "There won't," she promised.

The superintendent turned to Wally again. "*Gymnastics,*" he said.

Wally missed it. He put a *k* after the *c,* but when he walked offstage and the girl behind him was declared the winner, his shoulders were straight and his head erect, and he looked like a man released from prison.

"Caroline, how *could* you?" Mrs. Malloy whispered

angrily across Eddie's lap. "You ruined his chance to go to the state contest!"

And Caroline realized she had done it again—embarrassed her family. She had stood up before the largest audience she had ever faced and blown it. Nobody clapped and cheered. Nobody threw flowers. They hated her, and she deserved it. Her family was not proud of her in the least, and certainly neither were the Hatfords. Even Peter was scowling at her, and when the contest was over at last and both families moved toward the aisle to leave, Peter whispered to Caroline, "You are in deep, deep doo-doo."

Twenty

■

Apology

The only time Wally could remember being so relieved was the time he thought he'd broken his leg but had only sprained it. He had been all ready to misspell a word on purpose, but he really had not known whether *gymnastics* had a *k* near the end or not.

He could not get off the stage fast enough, but as he took his place in the second row and glanced behind him, he noticed Beth and Eddie with their hands over their faces and knew that Caroline was in trouble.

But he could not have felt better himself. Not only had he kept Caroline from going to the state contest and being so stuck-up they couldn't stand her, but her outburst had made her whole family angry with her.

It wasn't until he looked back over his other shoulder, however, that he saw the disappointment in his parents' faces. And suddenly he discovered that he had blown the one thing he was really good at. Nobody seemed to know he was around until they wanted something spelled. When Josh or Jake was writing a report and needed to know how a word was spelled, he'd usually call out to Wally instead of using the dictionary.

"Hey, Wally, does *judgment* have an *e* after the *g*?" Josh might say.

Or Jake would call, "Wally, does *Connecticut* have one *t* at the end or two?"

Even his parents asked him to spell a word now and then.

But just because he was a good speller, did that mean he had to worry all the way through Buckman Elementary that he would have to go to the county contest? If he won the county contest, he'd have to worry about going to the state, and if he won that, he'd worry about going to the national! What did his parents expect of him, anyway? To become President of the United States?

When he joined his family later, his mother put her arm around his shoulder and said, "That was such a shame about Caroline, Wally. I think she got you rattled. You *should* have been the winner."

"No, it's okay," Wally said. "You know how I feel about contests."

His dad patted him on the back. "Well, no one else in the family ever got as far as a county spelling bee, son. We're right proud of you."

"Thanks, Dad," said Wally. It *was* nice to be noticed for a change. By his family, anyway.

As everyone moved toward the center aisle, Wally

noticed that Caroline seemed to be trying to get out of the auditorium as fast as possible, but Coach Malloy's big hand reached out, grabbed her shoulder, and hauled her backward a few steps until she was face to face with the Hatfords.

"Wally," said Coach Malloy. "I think my daughter has something to say to you."

"I—I'm s-s-sorry," Caroline stammered.

"For what?" her father demanded.

"For—for trying to help Wally," said Caroline.

"No, that is not what you were trying to do," Coach Malloy said.

"For—for . . ." Caroline's face suddenly looked like a squished tomato as her eyes crinkled up, and Wally *almost* felt sorry for her. "For—for . . . trying to take his p-place in the contest."

"Right," said her father. "You embarrassed us, you embarrassed Wally, and you embarrassed yourself." He turned to Mr. and Mrs. Hatford. "I hope you can understand how upset we are with our daughter."

"Yes," said Mrs. Hatford. And then she added, with a little smile, "I never raised a daughter, but I do understand."

Then she and Caroline's mother chattered on about other things, and Wally's brothers grinned and elbowed him as they left the auditorium and stepped out into the sweet April air.

Twenty-one

■

What Caroline Saw

It was a quiet and subdued Caroline who came down to breakfast Sunday morning. She kept her eyes on her scrambled eggs all the while she ate and said "Yes, please" and "No, thanks" when offered toast or bacon.

No one said anything more about what had happened at the spelling contest. It was obvious to the entire family that Caroline had been mortified and had suffered enough. For once in her life she had seen herself as others saw her and hadn't liked what she'd seen.

When everyone else had left the kitchen except Caroline and Mrs. Malloy, Caroline squeaked, "I'm—I'm really sorry about last night, Mother."

"So am I," said her mother. "But if you learned something from it, Caroline, perhaps it wasn't entirely wasted. To be a great actress you must first be a great human being, and I think you need a little work in that department."

It was a gray day all around. When the girls noticed the Hatford boys fooling around down by the swinging bridge, they put on their jackets and sauntered down the hill. Caroline was relieved that none of the boys mentioned the spelling bee either. Everyone in town, she decided, must know just how awful she felt inside. A drop of rain hit her on her cheek.

"Hey! Rain!" Jake chortled. "And tonight's the night the principal sleeps on the roof."

"But he didn't say he'd *stay* up there," Eddie reminded them, looking out over the river, where tiny droplets were making circles on the water.

"Right!" Jake looked at the others and grinned. "Who's in favor of sneaking over there about midnight to check up on him?"

"I'll be too sleepy," said Peter.

Everyone looked down at Peter. They had almost forgotten he was along. A look passed among them.

"You're right," said Josh. "We'll all be too tired to do that. Besides, we don't want to get in any more trouble, do we?"

The rain was coming down a little harder now.

"I'm getting wet!" Peter yelled. "I'll beat you home." He ran on ahead, and Jake said quickly, "Okay, don't say anything more to Peter about this, but who wants to meet at the swinging bridge at midnight and go over to the school?"

"I do!" said Caroline.

"Yeah, we want to go!" said Eddie. "I'll bet we won't be the only ones there, either."

"Besides," said Caroline, "I can't get in any more trouble than I already am."

"Wrong!" they all said together.

"Okay, midnight it is," said Josh, and both groups ran for home as the rain pelted down on them.

■

All afternoon the girls shot glances at each other whenever they heard thunder or when the rain came down even harder for a spell. But at dinner they were surprised to hear their father say, "I suppose you girls are thinking of sneaking out tonight to see if your principal is still on the roof."

Caroline stopped chewing. She looked across the table at Beth and Eddie, who had stopped chewing also. Their father smiled a little.

"Oh, don't think I don't know what goes on in those heads of yours. Tom Hatford says they're posting an officer at the school tonight, just in case some crazy kids decide to carry off the principal's ladder or climb up on the roof to see if he's there."

"Well, I'll bet he's not, with all this rain," said Beth.

"Tell you what," her father said. "If you *do* go over there, I want you to go as a group and come back as a group. Eddie, I expect you to see to that. Go with the Hatford boys and don't do anything stupid. Got it?"

"Okay," said Eddie, and looked at her sisters in surprise.

Somehow it didn't seem as much fun, sneaking out at midnight with permission, Caroline thought.

Still, how often did her father allow her to stay up until midnight, much less *go* somewhere at that hour?

All evening the girls watched the clock and listened to the rain, which kept up a steady drumming. Around nine they got a call from the Hatfords.

"Hey, Caroline," said Josh. "Our dad talked to your dad, right?"

"Yeah," Caroline said.

"Well, you didn't exactly promise it would be midnight, did you?"

"No," said Caroline.

"We didn't either. And we figure that any other kids who show up will come at midnight or before. So why don't *we* go at one o'clock?"

Caroline wasn't sure if she could stay awake that long, but she checked with her sisters.

"No problem," she said, getting back to Josh. "Eddie says we'll met you at the end of the swinging bridge at one."

"See you," said Josh, and he hung up.

To stay awake the girls got out some cards and played speed, then crazy eights, then hearts, then spite and malice. Their parents were in bed by eleven. At five minutes to one the girls went outside to check the weather and found that it was not only still raining, but pouring. They put on their boots and hooded raincoats, then left the house with a flashlight and slogged their way down the hill to the bridge and over the swaying boards to the other side, where the Hatford boys, all but Peter, were waiting.

"Is your dad on duty at the school?" Caroline asked.

"No, they've got a rookie making regular stops at the school to see that everything's okay," Wally said.

It was raining so hard that Caroline felt like a duck. Everything squished—her socks, her shoes, her boots, the rubberized sleeves of her raincoat. She almost felt as though, if she flapped her arms, she would quack.

As they walked the two blocks to the school, however, the rain began to slack off, and by the time they got there, it had stopped entirely. Still, their effort was hardly worth it, for just as Wally had said, they noticed a policeman sitting in a squad car at the edge of the playground, watching the building. One outdoor light shone above the front entrance. There was a big sign at the bottom of the ladder to the roof saying KEEP OFF and a banner waving from the rooftop that read YES, THE PRINCIPAL IS HERE. There was no way to check, with a policeman there. Besides, the sign was probably right. No one was going to be able to climb up on the roof, and they might as well go back home.

"Well, I guess that settles that," said Beth.

"Heck," said Wally. "This isn't any fun."

But Josh put one finger to his lips, and they all crept closer to the squad car, keeping to the shadows.

The rookie, Officer Clay, was talking on his police radio to someone back at headquarters: "Yeah, I think we can wrap it up for the night. Kelly's sound asleep up there, and nobody's been by for the last forty minutes or so. I think the rain's put a damper on things, lucky for us. . . . Okay, I'll drive by every half hour, but I think we'll have a peaceful night. . . . Sure, I'll do that. . . . Roger."

The seven kids stood dejectedly back in the bushes and watched Officer Clay drive away. The headlights made a wide arc across the playground as the car turned and headed toward the street.

"This is a bummer!" said Jake. "He's up there, all right."

"We're all dressed up with no place to go," said Beth.

"Well, there's nothing to say we can't take the long way home," Eddie suggested. "We could walk into the business district and see if they've changed the movie for next week."

"Yeah, we could check the ice cream shop, see if they've posted the new flavor for May," said Wally.

"Or go as far as the bookstore and see what books Mike Oldaker has in his window," said Beth.

They turned and trooped back down the bush-lined path leading out to the sidewalk, but Caroline, who was last in line, saw something out of the corner of her eye that made her stop. She stared through the darkness until she was sure she saw what she thought she had seen.

"Wait!" she whispered to the others.

Everyone turned, but when they saw Caroline motioning quickly for them to come back, they crowded around her, not making a sound.

What everyone *thought* they might see was the principal crawling out of his tent on the roof and sneaking down the ladder to go home. What they saw instead was two men creeping around the corner of the school building and making their way over to the ladder.

"Whoa!" whispered Jake. "What have we *here?*"

"Maybe they're plainclothes policemen hired to stand guard over Mr. Kelly all night," said Beth.

"Then why would Officer Clay say he'd stop by every half hour?" Eddie questioned.

None of the kids made a sound as one of the men began to climb the ladder and the other man looked around nervously below. From behind the bushes the Hatfords and the Malloys watched with open mouths as the man on the ladder reached the roof, climbed on, and made his way over to the tent.

"Do you think we should yell and wake up Mr. Kelly?" Wally asked.

"If it's a plainclothes policeman just wanting to make sure he's all right and we wake up the principal, we'll probably have to spend another day cleaning toilets at the police station," said Caroline.

"I don't know," said Beth, sounding uneasy. "What if they're going to hurt him?"

"Why would they do that?" Wally wondered aloud. But then he said, "If it looks like a fight, we'll yell that the police are on the way."

There was just enough light in the sky, now that the rain had stopped completely and the moon was out, to see the man on the roof get down on his hands and knees and crawl halfway inside the tent. A minute later he slowly backed out, and when he stood up, he appeared to be holding a pair of trousers. He waved them at the man on the ground below.

"He's got the principal's pants!" breathed Wally. "They're going to steal his clothes!"

But it didn't seem to be the pants the man wanted. He put his hand in one pocket of the pants and then the other. Finally he waved something shiny at the man on the ground below, put the trousers back in the tent, and climbed back down the ladder.

"Shhh," Jake warned the others. "Don't let them know we're here. Let's see what they do next."

What happened next was that the men went around to the front entrance of the school and, with the shiny something they had taken from the principal's pants— keys—they opened the door, closed it noiselessly behind them, and disappeared inside.

Twenty-two

■

And the Winner Is . . .

"I'll bet they're going to rob the school!" Jake said excitedly. "Did anyone get a good look at either of them?"

"One had dark hair," said Caroline.

"No, he was wearing a cap," said Eddie.

"He was short," said Jake.

"He was tall!" said Beth.

"They were both tall," said Caroline.

"No, they weren't. One was tall and one was short," said Eddie.

"And one was fat," said Caroline.

"They both were fat," said Josh.

Jake flung back his head. "What kind of witnesses *are* we, anyway?"

"Well, they were both wearing white Nikes," said Wally.

Everyone turned and stared at him.

"How do you know *that*?" asked his brothers.

"I just paid attention," said Wally.

"Should we climb up there and wake the principal?" asked Beth.

"No," said Josh. "What if they've got a gun? Officer Clay won't be back for a half hour. We've got to go home and get Dad."

Suddenly the hour after midnight seemed about as exciting as it could get. They all ran back out to the street and raced to the Hatfords' house. After Jake let them in with his key, he said, "Wally, go upstairs and wake Dad."

"What?" said Wally. "Why *me*?"

"Just because," said Jake. "Josh and I are going to write down all the different things we think we saw, and we have to do it while our memories are still fresh."

It always happened this way, Wally thought. He always seemed to get stuck with the stuff nobody else wanted to do. It might be exciting telling Dad about the man stealing the principal's keys, but it sure wouldn't be any fun waking him up. Their father was a deep sleeper, and if anything except a police beeper woke him up, he was liable to be grouchy.

Wally went up the stairs, stepping extra hard on the second from the bottom step, which always made the loudest squeak, hoping that might wake his dad.

His parents' door was closed, and he tapped lightly

once. Then twice. When nothing happened, he knocked really hard.

The bed squeaked, like someone turning over; then he heard his mother's voice: "Who is it?" She sounded sleepy.

"It's Wally," he said, and opened the door a crack. "Can I come in?"

"What's the matter, Wally?" she asked.

Wally came over to the bed. "The Malloy girls are downstairs," he said. "Caroline saw something. We all did."

Mrs. Hatford rose up on one elbow. "What do you mean, Caroline saw something? You know the imagination that girl has! Wally, it's almost two in the morning!"

"We saw some men go in the school."

Mr. Hatford gave a loud grumbling snort. "Whuzzat?" he said.

"It's Wally, dear," said his wife. "All the kids are downstairs, and they think they saw something." She turned back to Wally. "So how do you know they weren't teachers?"

"I don't. But they sneaked up on the roof after Officer Clay left and took the keys from the principal's pants. We watched them. Then they took the keys and went inside the school."

Mr. Hatford threw off the covers and swung his feet over the side of the bed.

"Where are they now?"

"They're still in the school, I think."

Wally's father reached for his robe and, with Wally and Mrs. Hatford behind him, hurried down the stairs to the kitchen, where the other kids were sitting. He bellowed like a bull when none of the six could give him a good description of the men but was pleased that Wally had noticed their white Nikes.

Everyone listened as they sat around the kitchen table with Mr. Hatford as he made a call on his police radio.

"Bogdan?" he said. "My kids say two men stole the principal's keys and are over in the school right now. Do you read me?"

The police radio crackled. "Roger," said Sergeant Bogdan. "Officer Clay is only two blocks away from the school right now. I'll send him over."

"You may need a backup," said Mr. Hatford. "My guess is they're after the computers. I can be there in three minutes."

"Won't be necessary. I've got Frank only a mile away. We've got it covered. Stay right there, Tom. We may want more information from those kids."

Mrs. Hatford made cocoa for everyone while Jake and the others described everything they had seen. Minutes went by.

Then the radio crackled again.

"Can the kids give us a good description of the men?" asked Sergeant Bogdan.

"Fat, thin, tall, short, dark hair, cap . . . you

name it," said Mr. Hatford. "No two of them can agree. But both men *were* wearing white Nikes."

There were the sounds of several voices now. Officer Clay's radio was transmitting as well. There were shouts. More noise. More shouts. And finally Officer Clay announced that he and Frank Miller had cornered two men in the computer room in the school library and had them under arrest.

"So what have you got?" Mr. Hatford asked.

This time Frank Miller answered. "Well, there are two middle-aged men, medium height, pudgy, white—"

"What about hair?" asked Wally's father.

"Both of 'em bald as a cue ball," came the answer.

Mr. Hatford laughed. "So much for the star witnesses."

"But one had on a cap," said Officer Clay.

"I *said* he was wearing a cap!" said Eddie.

Now it was Sergeant Bogdan again. "You said Caroline Malloy saw him first. Is she still there, by chance?"

"Yes," said Mr. Hatford.

"Put her on, would you?"

Mr. Hatford showed Caroline how to use the police radio.

"Hello?" she said.

"Good job, Caroline," said Sergeant Bogdan. "You've got a sharp eye to catch what you saw in the dark, and saved the school a heap of money. They had four computers all stacked up, ready to go."

"Thank you!" said Caroline airily, in as queenlike a

fashion as she could manage. But then she surprised everyone when she said, "It was the boys who knew what to do, though. It was Jake who said we should go get his dad."

"Well, all of you get the credit, then. I can almost forgive what you did to my police station," Sergeant Bogdan said, laughing. "You kids get some sleep now. It'll all be in the news tomorrow."

"But . . . but . . . shouldn't we stay up and wait for the photographer?" Caroline asked in dismay.

Sergeant Bogdan laughed again. "I'm not waking up any photographer over *these* two losers," he said. "I'll call in a report myself, but you'll get your name in the paper along with the others, don't you worry."

The next day it was indeed in the news. And when the Hatford boys and the Malloy girls got to school, there was the principal sitting on the roof in his pajamas, eating his Wheaties. He was reading the morning paper, which contained the story of all that had happened while he was asleep. Again and again that day Caroline and her sisters and Wally and his brothers had to tell about the excitement of the night before, and even Mr. Bailey asked questions about it at baseball practice.

After dinner that evening, as the Hatford boys were doing their homework around the dining room table, the Malloy girls rang the bell. Wally answered.

"We've got news!" Caroline said as the girls trooped in.

"Yeah?" Wally said. "What's up?" His brothers came into the living room, glad of a little break. But Wally didn't like the look in Beth's eyes.

"Guess what?" Beth said, hardly able to contain herself. "You know what day this is? The last day of April! And I just got a phone call from a man up near Philippi who said he found my bottle! So I'm Queen for a Day! Beginning tomorrow!"

The boys groaned.

"Yeah?" said Jake. "How do we know you're telling the truth? How do we know the bottle wasn't found right here in Buckman?"

"Because I got his phone number, and you can check with him yourself," Beth said.

"Okay," said Jake, "but how do we know that was one of the bottles we all started with? What did he say was in it?"

Beth's eyes narrowed with delight. "A matchbox cover! Right?"

Jake groaned again. "Right."

There was no getting around the fact that a deal was a deal and that Beth was now queen. The girls seated themselves on the couch, but the Hatford boys flopped down on the living room rug and prepared for the worst.

"Okay," said Jake, resigned. "What do we have to do?"

"I've made a list," said Beth, and pulled it out of her pocket. "If you think *you* worked *us* hard at the police station, Jake, wait till you see what I'm going to make you do!"

Jake looked helplessly around at his brothers while Beth began reading her list aloud: "Wash all my sneakers, type my book report, check my math homework, polish my toenails, mend my jeans, paint my bookcase, transplant my ivy, clean out my goldfish bowl, give me a perm, build me a—"

She was interrupted by the ringing of the telephone, and Wally reached behind him and picked it up.

"Could I speak with Peter?" a girl asked.

"Pe-ter! For yooooouuuu! A giiirrrlll!" Wally teased, holding the phone out in front of him.

With a quizzical look, Peter got up from the floor and took the phone.

"Ohhhh, Peter!" Jake cooed.

"Hello?" Peter said.

Everyone was quiet while he listened. Beth took the opportunity to scribble another chore on her list.

"Yeah?" said Peter into the phone. Then, "What?" Then, "Yeah?" again.

He stopped and looked at the others. "It's a girl," he said. "She just found my bottle. She was walking her dog."

"Where?" everyone asked at once.

Peter put the phone to his ear again.

"Where?" he asked. He listened, then said to the others, "Up near Tygart Lake."

"Tygart Lake!" cried Josh. "Way up there?"

"Peter, your bottle went farthest of all!" said Jake. "You're King for a Day."

Peter put the phone down on the table, a grin spreading slowly across his face.

"Hello?" came a voice from the phone.

Caroline grabbed it. "Hello," she said. "Can you tell me what else was in the bottle?" She waited. "Oh. . . . Yes, it's a button, all right. A Girl Scout button. Thanks." And she hung up.

Beth looked around the room in dismay. "But I had it all figured out. I knew exactly what I wanted each of you to do."

"That's the way the ball bounces," said Jake.

"That's the way the cookie crumbles," said Josh.

"Oh, well," said Eddie. "We have the baseball games to look forward to next month."

"And there will always be another time to be queen, Beth, though I don't know just when it will be," said Caroline.

"So, Peter, what do you want us to do?" said Jake. "We're your servants! Your slaves!" He knelt dramatically and touched his head to the floor.

Peter giggled. "Ride me around on your shoulders and I'll tell you," he said.

Jake waited while Peter climbed on, and, once up in the air, Peter took the yardstick Josh handed him to use as his scepter.

As Jake moved slowly about the room with Peter on

his shoulders, Peter touched each person on the head with the yardstick and gave a command.

To Eddie he said, "Bake me a double batch of chocolate brownies."

To Beth he said, "Bake me a great big giant batch of chocolate chip cookies."

"Peter, you're going to get sick," Wally warned, but Peter ignored him. He touched Caroline on the forehead with the yardstick and said, "Make me a great big pan of chocolate marshmallow fudge."

"What about us?" said Jake. "What do we have to do?"

Peter thought about it.

"For a whole day," he said, "you have to take me everywhere you go and let me do whatever you do."

"Easy," said Jake, grinning.

"You have to let me read all your comic books and play all your computer games."

"It's a deal," said Wally, thinking how easy they were getting off.

"I get to borrow your skateboards and your felt-tip pens and your baseball cards and your binoculars."

"Is that all?" said Wally.

"I get all your leftover Halloween candy," said Peter.

"Sold!" said Jake.

"And one more thing," said Peter, holding tightly to Jake's forehead so that he couldn't be dropped. "You've got to clean out my closet."

"No!" cried Jake and Josh and Wally together.

"A deal's a deal!" said Eddie. "Peter is King for a Day."

"That's the way the ball bounces," said Beth.

"That's the way the cookie crumbles," said Caroline.

About the Author

Phyllis Reynolds Naylor enjoys writing about the Hatford boys and the Malloy girls because the books take place in her husband's home state, West Virginia. The town of Buckman in the stories is really Buckhannon, where her husband spent most of his growing-up years. There are now eight books in the series—*The Boys Start the War, The Girls Get Even, Boys Against Girls, The Girls' Revenge, A Traitor Among the Boys, A Spy Among the Girls, The Boys Return,* and *The Girls Take Over*—and Mrs. Naylor plans to write four more, one for each month that the girls are in Buckman, though who knows whether they might just decide to stay?

Phyllis Reynolds Naylor is the author of more than a hundred books, a number of which are set in West Virginia, including the Newbery Award–winning *Shiloh* and the other two books in the Shiloh trilogy, *Shiloh Season* and *Saving Shiloh.* She and her husband live in Bethesda, Maryland.